Praise for Dennis Cooper:

"Cooper's work claims the bleakest regions of American afflu-
ence with the sureness of Faulkner staking out Yoknapatawpha
County. . . . [*Guide* is] the most seductively frightening, best
written novel of contemporary urban life that anyone has at-
tempted in a long time."   —*Los Angeles Times Book Review*

"*Period* is . . . heartbreaking. It's about loneliness and desire and
the ways in which they twist us in the great brutal nothing of the
American soul."   —*LA Weekly*

"Cooper's beautifully stark prose belies an effort of construction
in much the same way your favorite minimalist architect rules:
it's because he's so sharp on classical structures that he's able to
intelligently rearrange as if by whim, or accident. Or compare
him to Beckett, whose characters appear to go nowhere until you
step back to examine the afterbirth of a new narrative form. Of
course, Dennis Cooper does nothing by accident."   —*i-D*

GOD JR.

Also by Dennis Cooper:

GOD JR.

Dennis Cooper

Black Cat
New York

a paperback original imprint of Grove/Atlantic, Inc.

Printed in the United States of America
Published simultaneously in Canada

The author is very grateful to Cody Reding, Ira Silverberg, Joel Westendorf, Amy Gerstler, Amy Hundley, Judy Hottensen, Morgan Entrekin, and my parents.

Library of Congress Cataloging-in-Publication Data

Cooper, Dennis, 1953–
    God Jr. / Dennis Cooper.
        p. cm.
      ISBN-10: 0-8021-7011-0
      ISBN-13: 978-0-8021-7011-8
      1. Traffic accident victims—Family relationships—Fiction.
    2. Traffic accident victims—Fiction. 3. Teenage boys—Death—Fiction.
    4. Loss (Psychology)—Fiction.   5. Fathers and sons—Fiction.
    6. Sons—Death—Fiction. 7. Grief—Fiction.   I. Title.
    PS3553.O582G63 2005
    813'.54—dc22   2004065652

Black Cat
a paperback original imprint of Grove/Atlantic, Inc.
841 Broadway
New York, NY 10003

06 07 08 09 10   10 9 8 7 6 5 4 3 2

For Yury Smirnov

Contents

GOD JR.

The Crowd Pleaser

I work for a company called the Little Evening Out. We make children's clothing for special occasions. Our founder was a one-legged Vietnam vet. He passed away in '93. Thanks to him, all of our employees are disabled. I sit in a wheelchair, but my upper body works. I can also think and talk. If I were sitting in a real chair, no one would guess I have a problem.

It's my day to work the showroom. Usually I'm stuck on the computer taking orders. If it weren't for the Internet, we'd be dead. But sometimes people walk in the door.

"How can I help you?"

"My son needs something fancy for a wedding," says a good-looking woman with a small blond boy.

She points at the wall where we display the samples. "What is that, exactly?"

"A bee. We do school plays."

"I see. And that?" she asks. She means the red molecule. That's what we call it. Sometimes people pay us to turn their kids' drawings into clothes. That kid was two.

I explain what it's called and why it came into existence.

"You want to wear that instead?" she asks the boy, and smiles at me. "Well, you can't. Maybe next time."

"No," he says quietly.

I never look at the kids. It's too painful. Not even little kids like him.

"Didn't I see you in the paper?" she asks me after a thoughtful pause. "I did, didn't I?"

"You mean last Thursday's *Times*."

"It was a fascinating story," she says. "Very complex. We discussed it in my class. I teach ethics."

"What did your students think?"

"They decided you're a very cool father," she says. "But they're not sure you're right."

"I'm quote-unquote obsessed."

"As you should be," she says earnestly. "Whether you're right on this particular issue or not."

*   *   *

She studies the display wall and decides she wants the little black tuxedo. Marianne, who's learning-disabled and obese, does the fittings. So we're done. I hand the woman my card.

"I'd like to see what you're building," she says. Marianne is leading her and her reluctant son away. "Is it possible to drive by? The paper printed your address, so I'm assuming it is."

"It's fine."

"I'd like to bring my students," she says. "Do you ever give tours?"

"If you can give me some notice."

She waves my card at me. "I'll call you?" she says.

*   *   *

"Was she getting on your case?" Al asks. I guess he overheard us from the office. He lost his right leg in a boating accident. His son died young like mine, but in his case, it wasn't his fault.

"No, she wants to see the monument. She wants to bring her students."

"They'll love it," he says. "They'll be all gung ho."

"It's an ethics class. So maybe not."

"Kids love it," he says. "My kids want to start a petition."

"How are they, by the way?"

"My older girl just got accepted into UCLA," he says. "Which reminds me. She says she met your Tommy once. She says she recognized his picture in the paper."

"Did she say how?"

"No," he says. "I should have asked. I'll ask her."

"I'm interested."

"She likes extreme sports," he says. "I think that might be it. She goes to those X-whatever shows. I think she's even dating one of them."

"That's probably it."

"They're not bad boys," he says uncertainly. "It's just something new. Like soccer was."

"I used to think they were a bunch of lazy asses who were always stoned or drunk. I didn't realize that if a boy that age was happy, he'd seem coarse."

Al's eyes look sad now. He must think I mean Tommy. Maybe I do. "I'll ask her," he says gently.

"Don't worry. They're harmless idiots. She'll be fine."

"Sorry to mention it," he says, and starts typing.

* * *

We receive maybe ten online orders every day. People link to our site from disabled support sites. There's always some imminent wedding or school play or funeral, and we're a godsend to them. They don't mind that the clothes won't fit perfectly. They just need us to help them. They send us long, moving e-mails with their orders. I think most of them don't even have children.

"Excuse me?" asks the woman from before. She has wandered into the office. I guess the boy is still getting fitted.

"Oh, hi. This is Al."

"You're a teacher," Al says to her. "My wife's a teacher."

"Small world," she says, smiling. Then she looks at me. "What about tomorrow? I mean for the tour."

"I work until six."

"Of course," she says, and cringes. "I wasn't thinking."

"Take the morning off," Al says.

"I could do it in the morning."

"That's perfect," she says.

"But I should warn you that I'm not so good with kids."

"That's perfect," she says again. "It's a small class. Twelve students, if they all show up."

"Is nine o'clock okay?"

She nods happily. "I'm excited," she says, and grabs my hand. "This is a big, big help."

*   *   *

After they leave, the two Mexican guys who make the clothes get their instructions. They work in a small warehouse behind the office. We keep the windows closed because they always play their music. It's cheerful to them, but those trumpets drive us crazy. Our radio is tuned to a local oldies station. Al, Marianne, and I are around the same age, meaning somewhere in our forties. The Mexicans are young illegal guys. Manuel was shot in the back when his family sneaked over the border. He's in a wheelchair like me. His friend Jose claimed he was dying of cancer to get the job. One night his wife left us a phone message saying he lied about the cancer. She sounded drunk. Al and I wanted to fire him until Marianne started crying. So we never mentioned the call to Jose. But I like Marianne to worry we could fire him any minute.

*   *   *

Al tries to grab the phone away from Marianne. She backs across the office dialing. She wants to hear the Eagles. He's a country-music purist. I'm basically indifferent. We may look like poignant triplets, but our pasts have different soundtracks. Still, we share, or, in my case, shared children. Kids don't care about their songs the way we care about the old ones. Music isn't special anymore. It's a given. It takes itself and every kid for granted, and we bear the collateral damage. The more recent the oldies, the less we mind and the more we're in agreement.

"Request that song we were talking about a few minutes ago."

"What's it called?" Al asks me. "Quick."

"We couldn't remember."

"Alice in Chains?" Al says.

"That's the band. We need the song."

"Stop, Marianne," Al says. "We have a better idea."

"I'll fire Jose."

"No, you won't," she says, smiling.

I push the intercom button that sends my amplified voice into the warehouse. "Jose, to the office."

Marianne cups her hand around the mouthpiece. "'Desperado' by the Eagles?" she asks. Her voice could be easily mistaken for a child's, so we always have her make our requests. It almost guarantees a play.

*   *   *

Jose walks into the office. He's a small, wiry guy with a boxer's messy face and gigantic upper arms. He's always rubbing his quote-unquote cancerous chest

11

around us. It bothered me when I thought he was sick, and it's intolerable now.

I look at him. "You're fired."

"Jim," Al says sharply to me. He looks at Jose. "You're not fired."

"We know you don't have cancer."

"Yes," he says sadly, and rubs his chest harder.

"No, you don't have cancer. Don't have it. We know you don't. Your wife told us you don't."

"My wife?" he says. Then I see his lying eyes understand.

"But you're not fired," Al says. "We forgive you."

Jose looks at Marianne. "It's okay," she says meekly. "It's good you don't have cancer."

He looks down at the floor. He stops rubbing his chest and makes a fist.

I want Jose to cry. He cried at my son's funeral. He cried even harder than I did. It made me feel better at the time. If I could hug him, I think he would cry. When he hugged me at the funeral, I started crying. I might have cried because I thought someone who was dying understood. But I can't stand up and hug him without giving away one of my secrets.

"It's okay. Just stop rubbing your fucking chest."

"Jim," Al says.

I smile as warmly as I can. Jose looks up cautiously and sees my smile, then walks back into the warehouse. By now "Desperado" is playing. None of us has even noticed.

"What was that about?" Al asks me. He's typing again.

"Maybe you shouldn't make me think about Tommy." I look at him, then Marianne. "For future reference."

* * *

We close at six but will leave earlier with the slightest excuse. It's 5:05. Al wants to interrogate one of his daughters, so we're done. Al and I carpool with Marianne, who drives painstakingly well. She dropped her son, Wayne, on his head when he was born. It damaged his future, so she's always very careful with ours. Al's house is a pint-sized Tudor. There's a sailboat in his driveway covered with a tarp. It's the one that took his leg off. His daughter won't let him sell it. He's told me several times he wishes someone would steal it. I've thought of hiring one of Tommy's dodgy friends to help. I could sell the boat on eBay to help pay off the monument's debts. But we'd have to steal the pink slip, which would mean breaking into Al's house.

Before the accident, I was a real estate agent. I covered part of the Hollywood Hills and did very well. Back then I bought the property just north of ours and had the house razed. I hoped to build expensive condos, but 9/11 ruined the market, and the land has come in handy. I put a fence along the street and took out all the trees and foliage. I thought the monument would fit. My first contractor assured me that it would. But we've had to lose most of our yard, and it needs a little piece of my neighbor's. He's a widower who never set foot in his yard until I offered to buy it. It's a wasted half-acre of trees and mowed grass. He won't be reasonable. That's what started the ruckus with my neighbors. Before he complained, they used to tell me my son was another Frank Gehry.

*   *   *

Twice every Monday through Friday, Marianne's car inches by the spot where my Lexus hit a phone pole. I was pinned beneath some wreckage. Tommy flew through the windshield. Fifteen minutes later, we pass the public phone where he dialed 911. Some dispatcher took a call from an incoherent male. I've decided it was Tommy, even though we couldn't ID his voice. Twenty minutes after that, we pass a bus bench where his body was discovered by some strangers. I've passed these places so many times that he has almost been erased. Soon his death will lack illustrations or even much of a story. If that was Tommy's voice on the 911 tape, he couldn't pronounce what he knew. I know I should have placed him in my car wreck, but I've never told a soul. I haven't even told my wife. I never had to. With his head injury, you wouldn't live that long. You couldn't walk that far. Maybe a block, they said. So there was never any question. But I guess he was special. People seem to need tragic strangers in their lives. They'll superimpose tragedy when there's nothing to prevent them. Our company's modest success is an example. Whoever people think killed my son has disappeared into oblivion. I just decided that oblivion was deciding not to walk, fuck, go to the bathroom by myself, or want to do those things again.

* * *

Marianne parks her idling car in our driveway and helps me into my wheelchair. We're squarely in the shadow of the monument-in-progress. It used to resemble a concise roller coaster that had partially collapsed. In the *Times* article, it was described as a giant piece of inedible candy. Yesterday one of the neighbors called it folk art run amok. When the massive, arched castle-style door is added tomorrow, it should refocus yet again.

"It looks bigger," Marianne says.

"It's slightly taller."

She smiles and waves at the workers. They're screwing big puzzle pieces of red and yellow skin onto its crazy skeleton. They pause and glare back at her, probably because I'm late again with their paychecks.

"They seem mean," she says.

"They're just mad because I'm dicking them around. I'm the one who's mean."

"You were a little mean to Jose," she says.

"No, I was mean to you."

"You weren't," she says reassuringly.

"Then what would you call it?"

She smiles at me. But then she's always smiling. According to this show I caught one time on TLC, people with low IQs fill in their blanks with an exaggerated warmth.

"Okay, that's a little mean," she says.

*　*　*

I can roll myself up the front walk, unlock the door, and push it open unassisted. My wife, Bette, hears my racket and walks into the entrance hall talking on her cell phone. She clicks it off and gives me her "something's wrong" look. It always makes me think she's figured me out. I can walk a little. That's one of my secrets. I can walk across a room. It doesn't even hurt. I discovered that last month. I'm constantly worried that I'll jiggle a leg or wake up with an erection. I have to sleep on my stomach and monitor my body like a mime.

*　*　*

"Let's talk," she says, glancing at her watch. "I'll start. *Dateline NBC* is sending some people on Monday morning. Just to look."

"How did that happen?"

"They called Fred," she says ominously. "He told Jane, who told me."

"That's scary."

"I called NBC and talked to some assistant to someone," she says. "He said they were planning to call us today, but I fear their slant. So Jane and I are rallying the wives. That's where I'm off to now."

"That's definitely bad."

"You should pay the guys today," she says. "Call Fred and make nice. Ask him not to go into the drugs thing. Ask him to show Tommy that much respect. Say the monument should be weighed on its merits. He'll understand that. If you have to, mention his drinking."

"They'll find out anyway. I'm sure they already have or they wouldn't be interested."

"You know my feelings," she says.

"I know what they were."

"This is war," she says. "That's my feeling. Fred can go fuck himself."

"We're fucked."

"Possibly," she says. She checks her watch.

"A teacher is bringing her class by in the morning. I'm going to show them around and I guess answer questions."

"We should be videotaping these things," she says, and starts toward the street. It's sad. I mean to watch her walk away. I can barely remember how it felt not to worry when or if she would come back.

* * *

My contractor is outside the kitchen window. It's the end of the workday. He's washing his hands with our garden hose. It's easier for me to call his cell phone than struggle through the back door. His name is Bill Riley. He's the otherwise unemployed dad of Tommy's last and only girlfriend, Mia. He wipes his hands on the legs of his jeans, then unhooks the phone from his utility belt. When he sees my number, he lets himself into the kitchen. I'm at the breakfast table smoking a joint and writing checks. He gets a Budweiser out of the fridge and sits down across from me.

"Can I express an opinion?" he asks. "Father-to-father?"

"Try me."

"Tommy was a good kid," he says.

"Thanks."

"The other day Mia said if she was rich, she'd build her own amusement park," he says. "And you know why? Because she's playing RollerCoaster Tycoon. It's a computer game."

"I know the game."

"So let's say Mia died tomorrow," he says. "Would I mortgage my house to build her amusement park? No, because she wouldn't be here to enjoy it, and it's probably a whim."

"And you couldn't afford it."

"But maybe I'd say, okay, I'll build a skateboard park and call it Mia Riley Park," he says.

I've finished writing the checks and push them toward him with a force that makes me realize I'm upset.

"She draws pictures, too," he continues. "You could hang them on a wall, and they wouldn't look half bad. But is she Picasso? No, man, she's not Picasso. And I loved your kid, but that is not a good building. What kind of building has no insides? Even the Statue of Liberty has some rooms and a staircase. The only reason it's a building is because you were a real estate agent and you jumped to that conclusion. Any normal person would have had the drawing framed."

"There were thirty-seven drawings."

"Or made a book out of them," he says.

"Mia's the one who told us it was a building."

"She also said Tommy was stoned when he drew them. It's something a stoned kid would like. When I look at it, I don't see Tommy. I don't feel Tommy."

"So are you saying you quit?"

"Not necessarily," he says.

"Then I don't understand."

"I guess not," he says, and puts the checks in his top pocket. "All right, maybe what I'm trying to say is you shouldn't smoke so much pot."

"Well, you try living in a wheelchair."

"Maybe you wouldn't be in a wheelchair if you didn't smoke so much pot," he says. Then he stands up abruptly and heads for the door.

"You didn't finish your beer."

*　*　*

I like to sit around our deserted house wishing things were different. That's how I found out I could walk. I wished my legs could support me, and they did. Now I wish the monument would burn down to the ground. Or I wish I'd hired this company that designs circus tents to create it. I wish I'd thought it was a big enough deal to make Tommy's art into a costume. If he'd known I would grant his wish, he would have drawn Christina Ricci naked. From what his friends tell me, he just wished he'd been so famous he could fuck her. The space between him and fucking her was immaterial. That's why he broke so many bones. That's why he never would have been a Tony Hawk. Every loudmouthed jerk he called a friend seems to have known that about him. I wish they'd respected him more. Or I wish they wouldn't think I'd feel less lonely if they nit-picked him to death. Or else I wish I did.

* * *

I seem to be asleep on the couch. Bette is suddenly above me with a cell phone in her hand. I think it's an offering. I can see my wheelchair all the way across the room. I must have wished I could walk more than a couple of feet and given it a shot. She could have been there long enough to solve the mystery. That might be our lawyer on the phone explaining why my deception is legal grounds for divorce. I think all these things in a rush while I pretend to need a moment to wake up.

"It's Fred," Bette says, then carefully mouths the words "He's drunk."

I take the phone. Bette and I share a reassuring cringe. "Sorry, Fred, what? I was taking a nap."

"I said this is a courtesy call," he says.

"Thanks. We should talk more often."

"Mm," he says.

"Is this about the *Dateline* thing?"

"So you know about that," he says.

"Can we set some ground rules?"

"Some what?" he says.

"You drink, I smoke grass. If they affect our decisions, that's nobody's business, don't you think?"

"I drink," he says.

"You understand?"

"You're saying . . . I don't want to sell you my yard . . . because I'm a drunk?" he says.

"Let's say we're wrong. I'm an overly sentimental dad, and you're a property owner with rights."

"I liked your son," he says. "He used to play in my yard. He loved my yard. I love my yard."

"Exactly. You're a guy who loves his yard."

"Okay, Jim," he says, and clears his throat. I think he's going to cry. When people cry within a moment of mentioning Tommy, I cry, too. Even if they're drunks who don't mean it.

"Gotta go, Fred."

* * *

Bette pushes my errant wheelchair to the couch. She holds me by the belt loops, then slides my ass from the cushions into its more unstable seat. It's hard for her because I used to be a horny, jogging, gym-addicted jock. And it's hard for me to keep my legs completely limp.

"What did I miss?"

"That we're fucked," she says. "Make that raped."

"That's bad."

"Someone at Nintendo saw the *Times* piece," she says. "They're claiming we stole their design. *Dateline* is doing some kind of special on Nintendo. It's their whateverth anniversary. Our thing with Fred is just a wacky side segment. They didn't even know Tommy died. When I told them, they put me on hold. When they came back, I heard laughing in the background. They think the whole monument angle just makes it wackier."

"So Tommy stole it?"

"Possibly," she says. "I'm off to see our lawyer now. And I have a call in to Mia." She grabs her car keys off the pile of news magazines on our coffee table.

"Maybe it's good."

"Meaning what?" she asks.

"I mean, doesn't wacky sound like heaven?"

She silently mouths what I've said. I guess she's imagining what might have made her say that. It makes her frown and jiggle the car keys.

"Bette, look at me."

She looks at my legs. About two months ago, they finally lost their old masculine shape and started filling my pants like water. "Okay?" she says testily, and checks her watch.

"Just look at me."

She crosses her arms and glowers at my legs. "What am I supposed to be seeing?" she asks.

* * *

I've rolled myself into Tommy's old bedroom and lit a joint. He lived upstairs with us until his seventeenth birthday. Then we let him take over the den. He'd just moved his stuff down here a week before he died. Apart from a desk covered with old bills and blueprints, everything in the room is still his. Most of the walls are decorated with his posters. All but one shows a famous skateboarder doing his or her signature trick. When Tommy was sixteen, he rendered his head onto Tony Hawk's body with Photoshop. Bette and I blew it up into a poster. He told us we'd embarrassed him. But after he died, we found it displayed here with the others. It's the one where the skateboarder looks like he can't believe he's in a poster.

Just because no one really knows how Tommy died doesn't mean it isn't real. It's just hard for them to know and difficult to remember. I don't mean it's too painful for me. It's not like looking at a real kid. That's why I like to get stoned and look at this poster. Just because it isn't real doesn't mean it isn't Tommy. We got stoned together. That's what we did. We rarely saw or heard each other right. He wished he was this mostly made-up guy. Or he did when he was stoned once. I didn't know him well enough to say this isn't really him. When you're stoned and you see someone you think you know unbelievably well fly through a windshield, it's not real. If you stay stoned, it stays unreal. Even if this isn't really Tommy, at least he didn't fly headfirst through a windshield right in front of my eyes.

* * *

"Jim," says Bette's voice. She's behind me. I guess I fell asleep with a stack of Tommy's drawings in my lap. A bunch of them slid down my legs and fanned out across the floor.

"What."

"Mia's here," her voice says.

"All right. Give me a second."

"It's true," her voice says.

"What's true?"

"Tommy copied the monument from a video game," her voice says. It's coming from somewhere behind and below me. So I guess she's picking up the drawings. "Mia lied. She just told me."

"That's bad."

Bette places the drawings in my lap. She crosses her arms. I cross mine. We both look at the drawing on the top and let its nothingness sink in. It's not even well drawn.

*   *   *

When I roll into the living room, I see Mia hugging my wife. Or rather, Bette is hugging Mia, and Mia is barely on her feet. She was always Tommy's girl-friend. She smokes so much grass she got nicknamed the Ghost when she was ten. After Tommy died, she seemed bewildered by me. It's as though her mind scrambled my image in order to protect her. Tommy's friends realized their futures didn't need his imme-diate presence. They stopped calling us. I get mass e-mails from a couple of them. It's like Mia couldn't recognize me without a son. But she seems to see me now. I think she has just this very moment figured out that my wheelchair's not a chair.

"Mia, you're hurting her."

"Oh, shit," she says, and throws her arms back in shock.

"It's okay."

Bette smiles at Mia while wincing and rubbing one of her shoulders. "I'll get ready for bed," she says to me. "So you two can talk."

"Mr. Baxter," Mia says. She looks down at my legs and starts bawling. She turns her back and drops into a crouch. She splays her hands on the floor and starts wailing and swearing. If I'm not crying now, Tommy really must be dead. I guess his imagination was the last thing to go. My imagination must have been clinging to it.

"What?"

"I'm sorry," she screeches. "I just wanted Tommy to have a monument."

"Listen, tell me about it."

*   *   *

I'm watching Mia play one of Tommy's old video games. Its silliness has completely dried her eyes. Now it's doing something nice to me. I stood here the afternoon Tommy died. I asked if he wanted to get high, and he did. He was swearing and bouncing around on his ass just like Mia. I don't mind. I don't even mind when she wins some puny fight and grins at me. I grin back because I know she needs that. I don't even mind if I've built a monument to a bad, stoned idea that meant almost nothing in the first place.

"Shit," Mia says, and throws down the controller in frustration. "I thought it was on level four. It's going to take me a minute." She picks up the controller again.

"Is this a good game?"

"Not really," she says. She pushes and pushes a button on the controller. On TV, a goofy-looking bear dutifully throws itself against a gate over and over. "There. Okay, watch."

The bear runs through the now open gate. It skids to a halt on the edge of a cliff. It leaps off the cliff and barely lands on a floating wooden platform. It jumps from one floating platform to another until it reaches a second cliff. Then it climbs down a ladder into a woodsy area. A swarm of bees attacks it. It runs up a rugged hill swatting at the bees. It zigzags through a series of tall purple stalagmites. It skids to a halt. Directly in front of it is the monument. There's no doubt about that. The bear stands there looking at the monument until it seems to get bored and starts shuffling its feet.

"Can it walk around it?"

The bear perks up and walks slowly around the perimeter until it reaches its original location.

"Can it go inside?"

"No, watch," Mia says. She makes the bear throw itself against the door over and over. "Tommy thought if he couldn't unlock it, it had to be important. But it was only a glitch in his game. I told him that a hundred times, but he never believed me."

I grab a few of Tommy's drawings off the stack on his desk and compare them to the original. "That's what he drew."

"Yeah," she says. "Look, I have to tell you something."

"What's inside it?"

"Some stupid puzzle," she says. "Or a stupid maze."

"Did Tommy know that?"

"God, no," she says. "We'd get stoned, and he'd sit here drawing the supposed inside of it for hours." She pulls a spiral notebook off the shelf by Tommy's bed. It's been wedged into a crowd of old textbooks. Bette and I thought it was full of sketchy lectures. Mia shuts her eyes and shakes the notebook. "These are his drawings in here. I drew the other ones."

I look at her and the drawings I'm holding and the notebook she's waving until that vaguely sinks in. "Why?"

"Because I was bored," she says.

"No, why did you lie?"

"Because if you'd seen what he drew, you never would have built anything," she says. "But when you thought he did my drawings, you seemed so proud."

"Wait, he had nothing to do with these?" I hold out her ugly drawings and shake them. So I guess I'm upset.

She picks up the GameCube's controller. She starts pushing buttons. "Look, I'll save the game now," she says. "If you open it, you'll be right at the bottom of that ladder back there, and you can walk over here."

"I can't believe this."

"It'll say Tommy's saved game," she says.

* * *

After she leaves, I look at the cover of the notebook. I make a wish that Mia's wrong and my son is a Picasso. But I'm not stoned, so the wish doesn't work. The first thing Tommy wanted to find inside the building was a big skateboard ramp. The next time he drew the ramp, it was covered with gang-style graffiti and shaped like a pot leaf. By the fifth drawing, it looked like the Vegas strip tied into a bow. After that, he just started drawing naked girls. It takes me pages of poorly drawn porn to realize they're Christina Ricci. Then I roll myself around the house with the notebook in my lap until I find Bette sitting at the table in the kitchen.

"How was that?" she says without looking at me.

I lay the notebook on the table. She gives it and me a weary look.

"Have you looked at this?"

She slides the notebook to her side of the table and flips it open. She looks at the first several drawings and sighs. She turns to a page near the back. "Mia drew these?" she says, and shuts the cover.

"No, Mia drew the other ones. These are Tommy's."

Bette looks at me. "Perfect," she says.

"Yeah." I look away.

I hear her grab the notebook. Then I feel it hit my shoulder. I deserve that, but I roll myself away and toward the door. I protect the only thing I have of Tommy's that I haven't already killed or blown out of proportion. That would be me.

"Here I was thinking, okay, so he copied it," her voice says. "But maybe he drew it so many times because he wanted to caress it."

I'm going to cry. I'm almost positive I will. If I do, it'll be about her. Her and me.

* * *

Bette and I haven't slept together in a year. We blame how tired we feel after getting me upstairs. When Tommy died, we were prescribed cuddling by a specialist. But disabled sex wasn't the cure. It was after we bought the second bed that I felt my legs happening. I credit smoking grass. It maketh Bette to lie down without her slab of a husband. It maketh me to stand up secretly without her help. It taketh away everything that was important to us and giveth us back a little bit that isn't.

*   *   *

We're in bed. Our beds are close enough that we can easily pass a joint back and forth in the dark. She has it at the moment. "So how did it go with the wives?"

"They've wavering," her voice says.

"That's bad."

"I guess so," her voice says. She hands me the joint. "I'm done." Then I hear her roll over onto her side.

"Do you miss Tommy?" I take a hit.

"Not as much as I used to," her voice says. "What about you?"

"Horribly."

"I don't want to think about it," her voice says. She sounds tired and tired of us and tired of him. Her bed squeaks until she finds a relaxing spot far away from me.

I put out the joint. I slide my legs over the edge of the bed, sit up, and rise unsteadily to my feet. "I'm done, too."

*   *   *

I've opened Tommy's game. I just lit another joint. I played a few video games with my son, so I'm not a total loser. The bear is waiting for me to get stoned at the foot of the ladder. I can't remember how Mia got him to the monument. We can see it poking over a hill to the right. Between it and us are all sorts of dangers, both quasi-living and organic. I remember the evil bees. I don't remember the club-wielding ferrets. A bear should be able to beat them. They fill him with boredom and impatience, or maybe I do. I wonder what Tommy used to think. He must have spent a lot of time wandering awestruck around this level. I'm just a former real estate agent. I see cheap land, relatively scenic views, and a potential resort.

I make the bear run. A swarm of bees dive-bombs his head. He swats at them. They disorient us, and he runs into a ferret. That's my fault. Three ferrets surround him and whack away with their clubs. He's still busy with the bees. I don't know which of the buttons makes him fight. So I make him run away until we're lost. His life is a caption of five tiny honeycombs. My naïveté has reduced them to one strobing shard. When I stop to reorient us, he grabs his knees and wheezes. We can't see the monument or the ladder. We finally spot a cave. Since he's a bear and I'm a guy who can't take care of people when I'm stoned, we make a run for the entrance. The second we're inside, something whacks him and kills us. I save my progress and quit. It says Jim's saved game.

The Remedial Logician

A school bus drives slowly down the street. The driver's eyes are locked on the monument. They stay with it. I don't think he sees the car paused in his path. Its driver is snapping a picture. Now he hears the bus and honks. There's a crash. It sounds worse than it looks. Maybe four seconds later, a tow truck speeds into view from the left. Its driver inches by the collision, then speeds away. Ever since the newspaper published that article, our house has been a magnet for tow trucks. They patrol the street like taxis. I like to sit out here watching my son's death create a tiny ripple effect.

Bette is expecting a call from some psychic. He's famously popular with the dead. They use his brain and hands to write earthly monologues. Bette e-mailed him a photo of Tommy. From what I understand, he'll stare at it intently. Then Tommy's dead energy will read his mind and accept it like a ticket. I wanted Tommy's death to last forever. That's all. But Bette really wants him to stay. Even if he's incredibly abstract. Even if he's faint. Even if he's unbelievably dodgy. I know she's gone eccentric out of grief. But now that my plan has failed so badly, I'm rooting for hers.

The teacher brought her little son. He holds her hand tightly while the drivers trade licenses. Maybe five students stand near the damaged bus, squinting at my monument. They must not realize or care that I'm a few feet away. "Kurt Cobain only got a statue in a park," says one girl. "So why does this guy's son rate?" "When my dad died, my mom started drinking," says a boy. "I don't think that was ethical, because it hurt me." "Yeah, it's kind of arrogant," says another boy. "Walt Disney wanted to be frozen when he died," says another girl. "He wasn't, but I guess his family had a right not to do that."

We haven't talked about last night. Bette's eyes just seem flightier today. We're also out of sync because I finished off our pot. I've paged our dealer. Our lawyer phoned us. He says if Tommy loved a glitch in some video game, that's our spin. If Nintendo doesn't see a dad's devotion to his son as amazing product placement, they're fools. He has arranged for some expert to drop by tomorrow and compare all the monuments. His best-case scenario: Mia didn't nail the original, ours failed hers, and the construction crew cut a few too many corners. If so, it's called appropriation, not stealing, and I'm probably an artist.

The teacher's name is Julie. I didn't catch her son's. She just handed me a drawing he made. To her, it's a costume in vitro. He drew a simple head, arms, and legs. Then he got lazy and scribbled in the middle. I've seen hundreds exactly like it. In my year at the company, there's been only one boy who designed a custom outfit. He was so gay he might as well have been a girl. The rest wouldn't even try theirs on, which is why we have those samples. When boys are allowed to pick their own costumes, they always want to be something that someone else has imagined.

I lead Julie and her son into our kitchen. Bette is over by the sink holding the phone to her ear with a wet, foamy hand. When she spots me, she gives her conversation a wary thumb up. Then she notices Julie and her son. Something about them makes her forget what she's saying. So maybe Julie's the type of woman who made me cheat on Bette back when. I've been wondering about that myself. Bette really knew me once. Or maybe Julie's son looks too much like early Tommy. I can't exactly look, so I wouldn't really know. But he has sort of given me the creeps.

"What do you teach?" Bette asks. She looks out the window at the students who are touring the monument.

"Ethics," Julie says.

"No wonder they seem glum," Bette says.

"I taught art until the state cut our funding," Julie says. "Sometimes I think teaching kids ethics is like cursing them. But that's life."

"One of them reminds me of Tommy," Bette says. She looks back at me. "Doesn't he? I mean apart from the obvious."

I can't see the students from my wheelchair, but I vaguely saw the kid she means.

"Enough to give me a pang," Bette says. She looks at him again. "A little pang."

"Sparky Dole," Julie says without even looking.

"Is he a good kid?" Bette asks.

"Absolutely not," Julie says. "Far from it."

"That's too bad," Bette says. "He's the only one who isn't sitting in the driveway smoking a cigarette."

Julie's gone outside to reprimand her students. She deposited her son with us. Bette gave him a cookie, then left to check her e-mail. The psychic is sending us a Microsoft Word file of Tommy's speech from the beyond. I can hear it printing out. The boy is eating the cookie, studying my legs, and kicking his own legs playfully or cruelly. I'm trying to filter his mother's face out of his, but she's very ingrained. I'm just curious what kind of men she has sex with. So I guess I would have found her attractive. These days sex is so hypothetical and littered with stars it might as well be astronomy.

Bette walks into the kitchen holding a crumpled piece of paper. Her eyes are wet and disfigured from crying. I doubt whatever's written there originated in my son. I've seen the psychic do his thing on cable TV shows. I've seen him turn white then start typing frantically on a laptop. I've watched people cry when they read the love letters he's typed. I think the trick to remaining objective lies in never seeing what he's written. I can't take the chance that knowing Tommy's finally gone will make me cry. I want him to be something I'm vaguely scared will make me never feel a thing again.

"So you think the letter's real?"

"How could he know these things?" Bette says. She absentmindedly holds out the page, then withdraws it. "Oh right, you're scared."

"What things?"

She smiles at Julie's son. "Do you believe in ghosts?"

"My dad's a ghost," he says.

"That's interesting," she says. "Do you talk to him?"

"He protects my mom," he says, and sort of smirks at me. It makes Bette look at me, too.

"What's your problem, kid?"

"Jim," Bette says sharply.

"This kid's got some kind of problem with me."

"It's okay, sweetie," Bette says to the boy. "Jim—that's my husband's name—and I lost our son last year. We're feeling a little unhappy."

"He's not unhappy," the boy says to her.

"He's very, very unhappy," Bette says.

The boy frowns at me. I frown back at him. "I don't think so," he says.

"I don't think you understand," she says, and looks at me. "But that's okay."

I've led the students into Tommy's old bedroom. I hoped they'd be waxing enthusiastic and pumping me for details. But I'm used to Tommy's loudmouthed, idiotic friends. One by one they shake my hand politely. A few of them look into my eyes, but I can't return the favor. An Asian girl takes a snow globe from the dozen or so on a shelf. Tommy collected them when he was twelve. She studies the crude plastic figurines inside the globe and shakes it. What made this globe collectible was the snow. It was fluorescent orange when Tommy bought it. Now it looks like an underwater ashtray.

"This is cool," says the Asian girl. She hands the snow globe to a towering black kid.

He shakes the globe. Its crude *Star Trek: Deep Space Nine* figurines are magically dirtied. "True," he says.

"Fuck, I've got it," says the kid who looks like Tommy. It's just his giant clothes and wiry build and long, blunt hair, but that's a lot. "I've been to that thing outside before."

"Well, we're pretty sure he made it up."

He looks at me with incredible amazement. I know that look. It was always Tommy's favorite. On Tommy, it was traditional. On this kid, it's a punch.

"No, man, seriously," he says. "I was there."

"Yeah, Sparky, like five minutes ago," mutters the Asian girl.

The other students crack up. Then a few of them realize I haven't heard the whole story and politely clear their throats.

He looks at her with incredible sincerity.

"No, that's not it," he says.

The students crowd around my desk and position their notebooks. I've laid out five of Mia's drawings. They're the ones I used as blueprints. Four show the monument from a distance, and the fifth is a close-up. The Tommy look-alike studies them intently. The Asian girl and black young man give them a glance, then start fiddling with their pens. A heavyset Hispanic boy barely looks at all. It's like he thinks they'll hurt his eyes. He turns away and hunches over his notebook, frowning and doodling. From what I can see, the doodle's nothing more than a growing black dot. It's like he's digging a hole.

"I apologize," Julie says. Her students are sitting in the dented bus. "In class, most of them were very pro you. I'm afraid you got the lemons."

"It's okay. Long story, but I don't even care."

Julie rubs her son's head. "You like the funny house, don't you?" she says to him. He runs straight into her dress and grabs some of the folds. "I think that's a yes."

"So can I ask you an unethical question?"

"Try me," she says.

"Do you want to get a drink later?"

Her eyes jet to my legs. Then I see her realize how petty she is, and she looks away.

"Mom?" her son says. He backs out of the dress

and glares up at her. When she doesn't look down, he frowns at me.

"I mean, what's the worst that could happen?"

"Mom!" the boy shouts. He starts punching her angrily but very lightly in the legs.

Julie grabs his arm midpunch. "We've talked about this, Timothy," she says. Then she turns and smiles at me. "I'd better not. My husband died last year, and my son has some problems."

"So I've gathered." I smile at him. "But he sure can draw."

Tommy's friend Rick is our pot dealer now. When he arrived, I was playing the saved game. So I lit up a joint and let him take a turn. He's a lot more evil-minded than either Mia or me. We tried to domesticate the bear. We gave him our values. Rick's on his feet, wielding the controller like a Taser. Animals are being slaughtered as the bear whips his clumsy bulk around in seeming fury. After every creature in the level is dead, the bear hops, spins, does cartwheels, and backflips all the way to the monument. Then he and Rick start kicking the hell out of it until I order him to stop.

What if this game started life as a very different product? What if it were a real work of art that would have changed the gaming world forever? What if it totally freaked Nintendo out? What if they spent millions of dollars to redo it into something more commercial? What if this monument was part of the old game that nobody noticed until it was too late? What if they just locked the door, rendered these rocks around it, and hoped no one would notice? Maybe it's a whole world in there like, say, Zion in *The Matrix*. Or maybe I'm just stoned and it's just a bunch of fucked-up pixels.

Bette is driving me to work. I told her I have to work late. She hasn't driven me to work since Tommy died. I haven't worked late since she realized "working late" was my cover story for fucking other women. She's either secretly suspicious or indifferent, I can't tell anymore. I guess I don't particularly care. My all-time favorite song is Led Zeppelin's "Dazed and Confused." I didn't know it was their cover version of an old blues song for years. By the time I found out, I was already a fan. After I heard the original, Zeppelin's copy seemed overstated and weak. But I didn't change my mind. I just decided I was weak for continuing to love it.

"So where to, Rick?" Bette asks. We're giving him a lift. In return, we get an extra sliver of his stash. He's slumped in the backseat trying to recover from a bong hit.

"Where's your husband going?" he mumbles.

"To work, like I said."

"Just drop me off there," he says. He sits straight up and rubs his face back to life. Then he leans over the front seat and looks at my legs. "Can I ask you a personal question?"

"Ask her."

He looks at Bette. "Okay, can he still get it up?"

She gives me an irritated look. "No, he can't," she says.

"That sucks," Rick says. "But maybe it's more peaceful."

"You adjust," she says.

He turns to me. "Do you still think about doing it?"

"It just seems like something I did when I was younger and stupid."

"I used to smoke crack," he says.

"Okay, why did you stop?" Bette asks.

"I didn't," he says. "I just stopped telling people I smoke it."

"So why are you telling us?" she says.

"Because I like to impress people," he says.

"I'd be more impressed if you said 'I don't smoke crack,'" she says.

"No, you wouldn't," he says. "You'd say, 'Oh, that's nice.'"

"You can't know what I'd think, Rick," Bette says.

"Yeah, maybe," he says. Then he looks at my legs again. "No, that's a good point."

As soon as I roll into the office, Al makes an announcement. Jose went home last night and shot his wife. She's in intensive care and not expected to live. If she does survive, she'll be paralyzed from the neck or shoulders down. Also, Jose does have cancer. His wife's just an alcoholic with a mean streak. Marianne had to drive his medication to the jail. He burst into tears when he saw her. He begged her to ask for our forgiveness. So we need to replace Jose and quickly. But it should be someone who's so horribly disabled I won't possibly mistake them for a fake. "Hey," Al says sarcastically, "maybe we should hire his wife."

Custom costumes take a week to reach the buyer. First Al scans a drawing and sends the JPEG to this one-eyed deaf guy in Ohio who used to make stage props. He sends back the specs within a couple of days. I just handed Al the teacher's son's design. He jitters his eyes at the drawing and says it shouldn't be a problem. Since our company survives on custom orders, and we don't receive them very often, I feel useful for the first time in as long as I remember. But I'm still the guy who ruined a bunch of lives. I can tell by the look on Al's face that I'll never make a dent in what I did.

I want everyone to listen, so I crank the radio. It's playing "Janie's Got a Gun" by Aerosmith. I hate Aerosmith, but I hate myself more. Luckily, our business has a rule against getting outwardly mad. It was in our founder's will. That page of his will is framed and hangs on the wall of our office. When one of us gets mad, he or she looks meaningfully at the page. That's the signal. Al and Marianne are looking at it now. I used to look at it a lot until I knew it didn't work. Our founder's logic was that suffering should be nobly contained within the sufferers. But then he died from a stress-related stroke.

Al can't be near me. At six P.M. sharp, he puts his PC to sleep and struggles outside. Now it's Marianne and me and a wall of wrinkled, unloved costumes.

"Can I ask you a favor?"

"Do you deserve one?" she asks warmly. She's like sun. It doesn't matter whether warmth is warranted or what she truly feels. That's why we have her interface with the kids. Al's one leg and my wheelchair freak them out. They seem to think she's just extremely fat and nice.

"Yes, I do."

"Of course you do," she says, smiling.

"If you mean that, can we make a stop or two along our way, and if Bette asks, will you tell her I worked late?"

"Bette told me I should always drive straight home or she would kill me," Marianne says. "I don't think she meant it."

"I think she meant she'd kill me."

"No, she didn't," Marianne says. She shakes her head happily. "Don't be silly."

"Well, just in case she did, let's pretend I worked late."

I see a therapist every other week. Bette thinks she's over Tommy's death and exempt. Today I give the therapist something. It's a messy little drawing executed in multicolored crayon. There are billions just like it in the world. I drew it when I was eight. I'm hoping the therapist might say it's a picture of God or something great and I should have been an artist. I've never known or even heard of a kid who drew that badly and grew up to be an artist. I read somewhere that when little boys make art, nine times out of ten, they try to draw a cop. Of course, when your son's been killed, it's different. You're allowed to believe you would have had a wild imagination.

I'm on the sidewalk when a college student taps me on the shoulder. He's recognized me from the *Times*. He wants an explanation for the weird thing I've done. It's only weird to him because I can't justify it intellectually. My dad went to junior college for a year. He thought more school could have chiseled a career from his loose awe of the future. He used to harangue me to study and edit my goals. My original goal was to be famous as an unambitious loser. I think that's why Dad thought it seemed okay to treat me like I was. At least he died never knowing that my idiotic wish to be undeservedly famous would come true.

Our lawyer is giving me a quickie in the Starbucks near his office. Sometimes he's just my sounding board. He knows I killed Tommy. We can level with each other, since he's a cold, strategic prick. It's like talking to myself. He thinks doing *Dateline NBC* is suicidal. It's not that he cares if word gets out. He doesn't care about me. He just thinks I shouldn't scribble on a classic. He can't believe I wasn't charged with Tommy's murder. He says it takes him back to law school. It's one of those fairy-tale hypotheses that live and die in textbooks. It's so rare he thinks I should do everything in my power to protect it.

Music is blasting in my stoned head. My mind is full of friends we never see anymore. We're feeling nostalgic, so I've cranked KROQ. It's playing a set of so-called nuggets from the '80s. Tommy happens to walk in the living room when KROQ's playing a song called "She Sells Sanctuary" by a band that I think was called the Cult. Tommy smiles at the sound and grabs an imaginary microphone. He can't sing, but he sings anyway. Somehow he knows the song's lyrics and how the singer swivel-kicked the air around him in the song's video. Of course, we know all of that, too, and sit in vague appreciation of his heartless, facile, throwaway performance.

"I know your son's not dead. But in a funny way, he is. I mean, he can't move or talk or analyze things, so he's not really in the world."

"In a funny way, he is," Marianne says. "I like that."

"So, in a funny way, he's like Tommy."

"That's very nice," she says, and nods enthusiastically. "Thank you."

"So where is Wayne, then? Do you ever think about that? Where are dead people? Are they nowhere?"

"I know where Wayne is," she says. "Every day I read a fairy tale to him. Once before I go to work, and then when I get home. I just know that's where he is."

"That's crazy."

"I know it is," she says proudly.

"Okay, so tell me this. Tommy used to play a video game. I mean all the time, apparently. So, if I played it for him now . . ."

"Of course that would work," she says.

"Except the problem is he's dead."

"Oh, that's right," she says, and chuckles. "I'm such an idiot."

"So I guess he wouldn't know."

"That's a tough one," she says. She twists her smile and thinks about it. "Well, maybe you could pray."

I can't believe that's Tommy's grave. The last time I saw him, there was an ugly hole right there, and no other grave could compete. Now it's just the same extremely smooth grass that squashes everyone. I realize he's squashed. But I'm so stoned it seems implausible. He liked bad horror movies. He really loved this one where Christina Ricci blasted from the grave and killed her grieving parents. He watched it so often Bette finally burned the tape. I know there are a million dead kids who never intended to do every stupid little thing they thought about. I'm just here to say I hope mine would have understood my mistake.

Our mansion is so plain and unremarkable-looking it doesn't even have a style. In real estate circles it's called a lump. I know Bette is home because I don't have amnesia. I struggle from my wheelchair, then walk cautiously over the rugged rock path to our door. I ring the bell like a stranger. When Bette sees me standing on my feet, she suddenly lets out a wail. When something finally hits you, that's what you do. When Jose leaned over and hugged me at Tommy's funeral, I wailed my head off. I remember how that scared the borrowed sadness out of everyone else. Except for Bette, who heard my wail and started wailing, too.

The Childish Scrawl

The bear is a jewel among millions in a broochlike world. Then he knows his name is Jim and his body's my little costume. He can tell those are trees, oaks, but he understands they're no more oaks than emeralds are rocks. The air is heavier than real air and slightly yellowed, like the water in a snow globe. When he walks, he feels how stoned I am. Still, he lacks an opinion on anything to do with feeling pleasure. It's all a given. Nor can he assess my inabilities, then buck me off like an irritable horse. He's a figurative shot glass, and I'm the whiskey of his consciousness. When he moves, my ideas slosh around and cause his legs to lope toward whatever I want. So I aim him at a grumpy-looking ferret in a Sergeant Pepper jacket and puffy clown pants who's guarding a random post-age stamp of sun-stained grass.

* * *

'Hello. Can you think?' The bear's voice is more in-nocuous, hoarse, and upbeat than mine.

* * *

'Don't come any closer,' says the ferret. 'No farther than that gray rock, or I'll be triggered to destroy you or be destroyed.'

* * *

'I'm new around here.'

* * *

'You're Jim,' says the ferret. 'Father of Tommy. Un-certain bear. Liar. You want to know what I recall about you when you were your son. And maybe something else.'

*   *   *

'How do you know all that?'

*   *   *

'I think you'd say I read minds,' says the ferret after a pause that strikes me as thoughtful. To the bear, it was more like watching a strand of hair be combed. 'You were unhealthier when you were him. I met him twice. Both times he killed me for health. When I die, you get well. Apparently, that's fair. Kill me if you think you can. But I don't think you could.'

*   *   *

'I have a theory that I want to run by you. This game is built on the ruins of a more advanced game. You know, like in Egypt.'

* * *

'It's interesting you say that,' says the ferret. 'Sometimes when I'm paused, everything is different. This becomes a crazy place. I stand here frozen and misplaced in that unpleasantness. I wasn't programmed to wonder, but you can't live through something like that and not wonder. This is a level full of rumors and myths.'

* * *

'What do you know about that building over there?'

* * *

'You've asked me that twice,' says the ferret. 'And I always remind you that everything I know lies inside an invisible splotch. From that gray rock, to that cliff, to that stump, to that treasure chest. Ask me about these trees, this dirt, and I become a genius.'

*　*　*

The bear's head has swiveled. His eyes feel hooked by a coppery, glowing something or other in the distance. He understands the glow instinctively. I need to squint to see a wooden chest, jimmied open and sparkling like a flake of some gimmicky cereal. It's nestled in something that resembles a meadow or unmowed yard airbrushed onto a rumpled bath mat.

*　*　*

'Is there anything else you can tell me?'

*　*　*

'Yes, if you don't mind,' says the ferret. 'Whatever this level was, should have been, or is, there has always been one law. Players are meant to spend maybe ten of your human minutes here. They're meant to enter through that cave up there, learn something from the plant growing on that cliff, climb down into this valley, open two treasure chests, maybe kill a few of us, and leave through the cave near that beehive over there. Between Tommy and you, the bear has been with us much too long. My program was simple, kill or be killed. I wasn't meant to live forever. I wasn't meant to think, consider, daydream, pontificate. I'm like an elderly athlete. This club I'm holding seems heavy, even if it isn't. I'm so bored. We all are. If you have any mercy, erase this game and kill us. We'll be fine. We'll come back fresh and stupid and what you would call cheerful. It won't be like killing your son. We won't wander around bleeding and confused.'

* * *

'Well, first of all, badmouth Tommy again and we'll shred you like a document. And second, I've got a few things to do first, but fair enough.'

*   *   *

We're standing on that meadow I described while I wonder what a bear with a human-sized IQ would do next. Even when my legs worked perfectly, nature was a vacant lot to me. It didn't matter if it was stamped with officialdom like Yosemite or had been trucked in from the sticks and rolled out on some blighted city block. I'd stomach my picnics and vacations by reimagining my environs. I'd wish away ninety percent of the rural graffiti, then pencil in a mansion or lucrative casino, preserving every sixth or seventh tree for effect. But I'm not a real estate agent anymore, much less the kind of tech head who could have rendered or deleted this sweet-toothed, idyllic spot. I'm just some fingers resting lightly on a cursor as it slides magically around a kind of Ouija board.

*   *   *

'I have a suggestion,' says a voice. It's so disembodied, splintery, and high-pitched that we think some bee or hummingbird is orbiting our head. The bear starts swatting and running in a circle, flattening the lintlike grass and flowers. 'No, up here. Don't think acoustics, physics, none of that. In fact, don't think at all. Just turn the bear's head until you see the cliff, then push and hold 'Z'.'

* * *

The bear scans the busy, shrink-wrapped distance until we spot something that might qualify as a cliff. To me, it looks like trash, maybe an old high-top shoe that some homeless guy has laced with drinking straws. Then we zoom in on the ladder that makes the bear see earth.

* * *

'Okay, now what?'

*　*　*

"Jim, we need to talk," says Bette's voice. We turn and see her standing in the doorway. I understand her weathered, shell-shocked face, and sense the cavernous, hostile maze of thoughts teeming inside her head, but the bear feels stunned by her utter lack of charm and the mess I've made of Tommy's room. Luckily, he's just a stupid idea I'm entertaining, so I manage to nod.

*　*　*

"If you still hear me in there, can you wait a second?"

*　*　*

'Certainly,' says the disembodied voice. 'Being paused is as close as we get around here to smoking one of your joints. Take your time.'

*　*　*

We try to walk, but my hobbling legs blend poorly with the bear's dexterous leggings. I aim us for the bed, but he wasn't built to sit in his dimension, much less here. So we tussle mentally until I figure out how to swing us around and face Bette. To the bear, she's a bland, nonthreatening character devoid of any prize. It takes all my concentration to fix our eyes on her.

"Leg problems," Bette says coldly.

"I'm in a zone, but yeah, that, too."

"Look, I want you to move out, at least for a while," Bette says. "We'll do *Dateline* together, and then that monstrosity next door is your problem. Because legally, it is. You know, you seem drunk."

"I look different."

"Since I don't even know who you are anymore, maybe you're just being you," Bette says. "But if you want to know the truth, you look crazy."

* * *

I tap my B button while the bear climbs the ladder. Then I push A, which heaves us onto the cliff top. We land squarely on a corrugated terrace. It's smeared with buttery moss and some tiny stained-glass lamps that the bear recognizes as flowers. Two stylized paw prints, evidence of some larger bear or passing Yeti, face a gargantuan tropical plant that someone or something has dressed in thrift-store castoffs like a scarecrow.

*   *   *

'I'm the brains around here,' says a voice from deep inside the plant. 'Nice view, yes? Have a quick look. Then plant your paws in the indicated dents and trigger me. Right now I'm just talking in my sleep.'

*   *   *

It's true, the view is kind of sweet. A tune of buzzing, grousing voices rings from the fjord, and the sky is so low and flat that I can pick up every brushstroke. The monument's little twin is the valley's skyscraper. Its curious crown, which Mia misconstrued as a trippy, abstract bobble, is in fact a crow's nest of the nautical variety, with barrel-shaped sides and what appears to be a hatchlike entrance in the floorboards. When I zoom in, I notice the hatch is flapping on two hinges like a storm-cellar door.

* * *

'I don't suppose I could jump onto that roof.'

* * *

'At the moment, no,' says the plant. 'Were you to play two . . . make that three more levels and learn the mega-jump, maybe. No one's ever bothered to come back here and try. Still, I've always wondered.'

* * *

'Are they hard levels?'

*　　*　　*

'For you, absolutely,' says the plant. 'You're the weakest bear I've ever seen. But trigger me, okay? Because you're getting my thinking at very low tide.'

*　　*　　*

I walk the bear into the appointed prints. The second we're aligned, the plant untangles its torso into something more flowery, then rips its blossom open like a Christmas gift.

*　　*　　*

'Need some help, Jim?' says the plant. It takes a deep, whooshing breath. 'And thank you. It's been ages.'

*   *   *

'You know what I like about this place? Well, almost everything so far. The constant stimulus is awesome. But then I'm a pothead in deep real-world shit at the moment.'

*   *   *

'Personally, I've always liked you bumbling types,' says the plant. 'You're the bears who keep me watered. But I know you have a million questions, so fire a few of them away.'

*   *   *

'Okay, I'd love to hear your memories of the bear named Tommy.'

*   *   *

'First you need to understand something,' says the plant. 'The bear is the bear. Your eyes are one degree livelier than the pattern on a teacup. You walk, you trot. You kill, you solve puzzles. There's just not a lot to you. We know you like a lion tamer knows a wooden chair. Meaning not well. That said, I'll tell you this. Tommy spent weeks and weeks right down there doing nothing. I say nothing because a stationary bear might as well be a topiary bear. All I know is what his odd behavior did to us. You'd call it maturity. We began to speculate. Why is the bear still here? He had no answers to give us, so we thought about ourselves. Why are we still here? Theories abounded. At least in this level, we saw the problem. In the other levels . . . well, it must have been hell. Imagine if you were born to spend ten to fifteen minutes interacting with a stranger and then he never arrives. Introversion was torture. For all intents and purposes, we're a handicapped bunch. I can barely move. I'm like Stephen Hawking if the cosmos were a zoo. Everywhere in this game, silly creatures and nerdy foliage became sophisticates. It was a plague. Word spread to the farthest reaches of this game about this bear that did nothing. Having the so-called luxury of seeing him, we kept our heads around here. But in other levels, where creatures had to daydream, the questions got mystical. What sort of bear possessed the powers to kick-start such an awful evolution? Well, a god, of course. So if you want a simple but not so simple answer, the consensus here is that the Tommy bear was God. See for yourself. Play the higher levels, ask around.'

*　*　*

'Did Tommy know all that?'

*　*　*

'That bear never asked,' says the plant. 'He was a gamer, and gamers always treat us like their play-ground equipment. We were polite and did our jobs.

See, we're in the bear's paws. If bears want a little something extra, they have to ask. I let that bear stew in his juices. I had no choice. I figured he was lazy or retarded or stoned or some combination thereof. But in the outskirts, they decided his inactivity meant God was distant and uncaring.'

*   *   *

'So what do you think is in that building down there?'

*   *   *

'I'm a logical sort,' says the plant. 'What nags at me is not what's inside. But why the balcony? What's the point? This is not a scenic place, as you can see. Those are my brain twisters. And before you ask, yes, like many here I get these mental pictures, very faint and suspicious, of somewhere uglier. Sometimes when we're paused, I'll have a vision. We all do. I'm here and I'm me, but the level . . . it's indescribable. A number of us think that's death. When we're paused, we're half dead, we're death looky-lous. If the bear ever wins this game, that's where we'll go. Or there's the déjà vu theory. What if it's the ancient past? I suppose I find that one slightly less credible, although it would help explain that balcony. Still, all that's so glamorous, and I'm not a wishful thinker. I think we're eroding. I think we're peeling away. I think this is borrowed time and that's rust. But you seem distracted.'

*   *   *

'Oh, sorry. I'm just thinking what if I played the higher levels and learned that jump you mentioned and managed to get inside that building? It's a long, long story, but I kind of need to know.'

*   *   *

'I'd kill for newness,' says the plant. 'Any slight change in here is like one of your world wars. So I encourage you. In fact, I have a suggestion. Next time you start the game, go to 'Menu' and choose 'Options,' then click on 'Diary.' You see, this game gives bears the option of keeping a record of their quest. No one's ever used it. It's rather unnecessary, to be honest. It needn't even exist. But knowing you a little, I think it couldn't hurt. I'm referring to your drug problem. Based on my limited experience, druggie bears forget. No offense intended.'

*   *   *

'This is nice, because in my world, I'm so stoned and depressed I'm pretty much useless.'

*   *   *

'I sense you want to spill your guts, but don't,' says the plant. 'I wouldn't respond if I could. Why do you think UFOs never land? Why don't ghosts just say hello? Next time you start your game, I promise I'll have spent my downtime stockpiling tips that will help you on your journey.'

* * *

"Jim," says Bette's voice. She's back in Tommy's room with a mysterious woman. To our eyes, they're red flags, but the stranger is the reddest, with tousled, gelled black hair and a juicy face I'd guess is Middle Eastern or Hispanic or just very, very suntanned. The bear in me finds her far more appetizing than Bette. His curiosity or hunger triggers a flirty look from me. That triggers a grimace from my wife, and it triggers the bear to fade away into her husband.

* * *

"Hold on in there." I pause the game.

* * *

"This is Malina," Bette says. "She's the . . . I'm sorry."

"Image analyst," the woman says. "Or digital orthophotography specialist, if you want to be technical about it."

"She needs to use Tommy's computer," Bette says. "So you need to stop playing with your little friends." Then she smiles painfully at the woman. "We've been through a lot."

* * *

I take the game off pause.

* * *

'You want to save and go,' says the plant. 'No problem. I'm a bit wiped myself. As I hope I've explained, the bear gets old fast. I have a fifteen-minute attention span, tops. It's genetic. Nothing personal. It's just that I've seen what I'm seeing so long I might as well be blind.'

*   *   *

Once the bear leaves my system, I feel normal, meaning rickety below the waist and rather jumpy above it. The alteration is complete and instantaneous. No hangover, numbness, nothing. One time a hypnotist snapped his fingers in my face. I couldn't remember why I'd volunteered to be an idiot. But I remembered lying inhumanly stiff between two chairs while some fat guy jumped on my stomach. The only real difference was the applause stung, whereas before it was just the world's spookiest wallpaper.

*   *   *

"It'll take me an hour," Malina says. She's seated at Tommy's iMac and is switching on the satellites that form its broad white shoulders. It's been a year since that screen saver loaded and Tony Hawk's hatchet face peered into Tommy's bloodshot eyes and yelled, "Eat me, bitch," over and over and over.

"Your family is quite a group of characters," Malina says, tapping down the volume.

* * *

Bette is sitting in our breakfast nook. One of her psychic's many self-published books is lying open to a glossy photo spread. It shows him bellowing or laughing in sequence while some dead person bangs his fingers down on a keyboard. Whenever I look at him, I see myself in spades. He's just more withered in the thighs and calves department, and his lies are bigger whoppers. Otherwise, I'm quite familiar with the drill. But thousands of widows and former mothers can't see through his silent movie acting and medieval leg braces.

"I'm still not used to you like this," Bette says. "But don't sit down. That's worse."

"So what's the latest on this psychic thing? I honestly want to know."

"He'll be here tomorrow morning, so you can see

for yourself," she says. "And I'll need to use Tommy's room again. And yes, it's going to cost an arm and leg. And before you get sarcastic, yes, your arm and leg."

* * *

I know the guy who squirmed in my wheelchair for a year killed Tommy, too. I know I'm still that guy with flabby legs and stilts for bones. I don't know why pathological lying seemed to make the world much simpler. I don't know why a false world made my son's death so inspiring, or why the real world is rubbed so raw because one lazy teen left it. I know Tommy wasn't born in a car crash. I know when I stood up, it didn't kill anyone. I don't know why I think standing up was the worst mistake of my life. I don't know why a bear that can't sit down is confused with the Almighty by everyone around him. I know why everyone in a false world would think a boy who spent his whole life doing nothing is God. I just don't know how to give it decent subtitles yet.

* * *

Malina's reached a verdict. It took her well under an hour. She's using some tricky software or other to give a slide show of her findings. It dawned with several screen grabs of the original building, then shuffled through the scans of Mia's version and is peaking with some recent shots of ours. Granted, pixels and painted wood are like diamonds and disco balls, but our monument looks so unbelievably deformed.

"Oh, thank God." I feel like hugging Malina, but that's not my style at all, so I thrust out my hand.

"In what sense?" she says. She studies my hand and sort of pinches it.

"Well, it's like God rode the Matterhorn in Disneyland before he conjured up the Alps."

"That's a colorful argument," she says. "Unfortunately, metaphors are inadmissible in court. I'm afraid the variations are minute." She pulls up a screen grab and aligns it with a photo. I look confusedly at Bette.

"Leave me out of this," she says.

"Look, that's a crow's nest, and that's some psychedelic nugget. And the colors . . . Ours are strictly business, and that looks like it's molded out of Jell-O."

"I promise you any judge will see double," Malina says. "You mentioned Disney. Well, it's like Mickey Mouse in the cartoons versus the guy in the costume who walks around at Disneyland. To us, it's day and night. But they're both Mickey Mouse, because children can't tell the difference."

"I'm shocked. To me, that's like saying a tree house is a variety of tree."

"I'm with him," Bette tells Malina. "But you have to understand, we smoke a lot of pot."

*   *   *

Jim's game, v.3, 22:14: As soon as I blended with the bear, we climbed the ladder and woke up our plant friend. It was so ecstatic to see us, I swear it almost tore itself out of the ground. I mean, assuming it could. It had devised a plan for us, which it proceeded to explain at an amphetamine clip. It sounded like an airtight thought to me, but then what do I know from solid plans? Briefly, the plant said we should pretend to be God when I played the higher levels. Since those levels' inhabitants never saw God, any bear would do the trick. This lie would save us from innumerable deaths and loosen what amounted to their tongues. Other than that, the plant gave us a general lay of the levels ahead and described their class systems so I wouldn't waste the bear's time grilling peons. I promised to come back someday and make the big jump. Then the bear went down and stood around the building while I tried to Method act us into an animal Zeus. I know it sounds insane, but this jam-packed, colorful little place is making me reassess some things about my life. For instance, there's so much dead space in my mansion back home. Every room could accommodate a conference and is so sparsely furnished with such unentertaining things. I'm referring to chairs for friends we haven't seen in ages, tables holding art books we dust but never crack, ethnic paintings and sculptures from our travels that quit resonating the minute we got home. Why shouldn't they hide wall safes or hold secret compartments full of jewels or drugs or money? I think when I move out, I'm going to rent a little cottage, then check out some novelty shops before I trek all the way to IKEA. When the bear's pose struck me as godlike, meaning sort of officious and lawyer-like, I walked him toward the exit. The ferrets appear to be supporters now, since they were extremely deferential. We walked too close to one, and I could see him borderline convulsing from the struggle not to club us. The bees hung politely by their hive like an asteroid belt. When we reached the entrance to the cave, I got nervous. The bear yelled, 'Are we cool?' into the blackness, and an echoing voice answered in the affirmative. We never bumped into whoever or whatever likes to hang around in there. We emerged unscathed, and I quickly saved my game as the plant had recommended. I would describe level four as a Saudi Arabian bazaar meets Boy Scout jamboree set in a stripped-down, weirdly glistening desert. Each of the maybe dozen shoplike tents was piled to the rafters with exotic tropes from the continent the game was simulating. The shopkeepers, whose car-alarm-like snores rippled the fabric of their big tops, were pygmy elephants, Dumbo adorable and all dolled up in fruity-looking sandals, robes, and turbans. They were deep asleep until the bear's shoulder clipped some sort of earring-meets-wind-chimes-type item. That woke up an employee, who took one look at us and trumpeted. I braced for an attack, but he launched into his sales pitch. Nothing on the shelves looked all that appetizing, and his schmooze was just a string of grade school jokes, but we decided to engage him in casual conversation. He was a pushy little pachyderm, by real-world standards. The bear seemed nonplussed, but then he's been equally smitten with everyone we've met.

As soon as the word God left our mouth, the shop owner was pretty much our slave. He told us that, just between him and God, the bazaar wasn't worth our precious time, but we should scour the desert for unusual rocks, then take a certain trail to some forsaken plateau where we would learn some sort of fighting move, smite an enemy, and win one new honeycomb of life. We thanked him and wandered for a few minutes, picking up and throwing rocks. Most went nowhere, but the golden ones shattered on impact, revealing little trinkets, which I assumed could come in handy. When we stepped on these trinkets, they were magically absorbed into our body and made a tinkling sound like when you enter a gift shop. Every time the bear received a trinket, he danced on his tiptoes like Muhammad Ali, and even I was happy. The quasi-desert was such a big improvement on real ones. Even the scorpions were cute as candy wrappers, and when they realized we were holy, they flopped right over on their backs. We must have spent an hour breaking rocks, punching holes in cacti, crushing scorpions, and everything we harmed or killed gave us a present. Eventually, the bear spotted the aforementioned trail. It wound up a parched, slightly wooden-looking mountain and proved quite treacherous. Still, thanks to our credentials, avalanches froze like awnings, and eroded sections of the trail reversed until they'd locked back into place. When we finally reached the plateau in question, the bear was winded and wheezing comically, but I felt like a teenager. I pushed him through a beaded curtain that I think was bougainvillea and found a hidden treasure chest, which he dutifully kicked open. It gave us a sledge-hammer that the bear seemed very jazzed to own. There was a giant drooping sunflower planted in one corner of the plateau, and I let the bear attack it several times. On the fourth blow, it came to life à la the plant one level back, exposing a black male face camouflaged into its calyx. The flower unfurled one leafy arm, which flexed a bulging, tattooed bicep. It was cradling a basketball-like seed that started bouncing on the ground. Then the sunflower taught us a move it called the dribble. Basically, the bear jumps, and when he's in midair, I push and hold the R button, which makes him slam the earth so hard it buckles slightly. The sunflower said this move would save our life. Being God, I guessed our thanks were merely an indulgence, but maybe ten seconds afterward, the bear was swallowing my pride. It seems that by testing out this move, we'd disturbed a sleeping snake. It rose dramatically from a giant crack we hadn't seen, complete with so much billowing, dry-ice-like dust it made a Cure concert seem hygienic, until the snake's massive checkerboard body towered far above our head. It bared two gooey fangs and glared down with these gyrating, laserium-like eyes. We immediately told him we were God. For a moment, the snake seemed startled that the bear could improvise, but then he countered that he didn't buy the cult religion sweeping through the level, and as far he cared, the bear was just a decent meal. Then he reared way back and kind of whipped us, which flattened the bear and reduced our health by several honeycombs. The bear wanted me to get his ass the hell away from there, but I was sure that any sign of weakness would result in vicious gossip. So I picked us up, brushed him off, and forced him to let me call the snake's bluff. Then I explained how I'd made the world out of this stuff called computer code and could so easily delete him. We said I admired his courage, and the bear found his puny strength amusing, but enough was enough. He was to give us our new honeycomb this second, or I would have him re-rendered as a non-golden rock or something even worse. I don't know how evolution works here. I don't know if I, a simple human guest, can read these creatures' eyes, but I thought I saw some doubt temper the snake's. So we kept threatening him until he said fine, he'd show us how to kill him. We were to do one of the dribbles. That would widen the crack he called home. After the fifth dribble, the plateau would break loose and crash onto the desert below, ending him. We'd lose some health in the tumble, but we'd survive. His corpse would be split almost in half. We'd notice a honeycomb digesting in his stomach. It would be ours to enjoy. So we did as he instructed, and sure enough, the bear wound up lying in the desert, disoriented but healthier than ever. I must admit I felt a form of sorrow for the kindly sunflower. It had gotten caught in the crossfire. The fall had mangled its petals and snapped its stem in several places. Still, it was sweet enough to feebly direct us to the cave that led to level five before it croaked. We found the cave without too much further hassle, then sweet-talked its inhabitants—bats, I'd guess, based on their piercing, eerie voices—with some God rhetoric, and made it through the dark without a scratch. When the next level dawned, it was close to ten-thirty P.M. my time, so I gave the game a break, saved the bear's progress, and typed out this entry, for whatever good it does. Good night.

*　*　*

I'm brushing my teeth. Bette is through with hers and flossing in a hurry. Then we'll go our separate ways. We put in twin Kohler sinks so we could brush our teeth together. In the old days, we'd slash at our faces and flirt in the mirror until we looked more like Santa Claus than us. After my accident, half the vanity was lowered and rebuilt into a wheelchair-friendly counter. I'd go about my business and wince up at her reflection. She'd pretend she could see me, wincing like a bad mother. Now that I can stand, my sink's so low I have to cower.

*　*　*

"Not that it matters anymore, but someone from *Dateline NBC* called," Bette says. "They canceled our segment. They decided it was too quirky."

"So is that good or bad news?"

Bette snaps the floss from one tight crevice and saws it down the next. "Look at yourself, Jim," she says.

I was already looking, but I hadn't cropped her out, which I guess is what she's asking.

"I look like I've been smoking pot and playing a video game for eleven hours straight."

"Deeper," she says.

"Okay, I look like my son's dead, and I've lost it."

"And you can walk," she says.

"Yeah, vaguely."

"Now think about it," Bette says. "Do you seem sympathetic? No, you don't, and let's get real. Do you think I can protect you now? It's very, very good news."

"So you mean I should move out."

"Oh, I almost forgot," she says. "There's bad news, too. Al called. He said to tell you Jose's wife died, and he's sorry, but they have to let you go. Poor guy. He was crying. He feels horrible about it. But I told him he shouldn't."

"I've been thinking. Maybe I could camp out in

the monument. I could sort of fix the place up. You know, turn a mountain into a molehill."

"I was thinking farther away," Bette says. "Like maybe in another dimension."

*   *   *

I took a stroll before I crashed. When your legs have amnesia, you have only two choices. You either torture them until they pretend they remember you, or you show them the world and hope they magically ignite like an infant's. I did one trudging lap around the monument. Then I saw Fred drinking on his patio and lumbered to the chain-link fence between our properties. It's been a while since I've seen his yard at night. When the sun's out, it's just another wilderness brochure. But the gardener has rigged up all these flood lamps with brightly colored gels. It reupholsters every plant and blade of grass and deck chair into something much trippier or more cohesive. If the bear weren't trapped in Tommy's room, I might try climbing the fence.

"Evening."

"You can walk," Fred says. "You walk better than I can." He raises his glass in a shaky toast.

"I guess you heard the *Dateline*'s canceled."

"Yeah, I thought about it, and I told them to shove off," he says. "There wasn't any point. You won't get my yard."

"Bette said they thought it was too quirky."

"Your wife tells you all kinds of shit," he says. "Hey, Jim. You want to hear the last thing your kid ever said to me?"

"Yeah, okay."

"He said, 'You're going to kill yourself if you keep drinking like that,'" Fred says. "And you know what I said to him? I said, 'Do something with your life, then talk to me, you fucking pothead.'"

"You want to hear the last thing he said to me?"

"Not really," Fred says. "I'm just an ugly drunk. It's true, though. Last thing I said to him."

"We were driving around. Tommy was going on and on about something he thought was really great. I think it was something that had happened to him. I wasn't really listening. But I didn't interrupt him, and I guess I usually did. I was thinking about something that made me happy. I don't remember what it was. But I guess I looked happy, and I guess he thought he'd made me happy. So he stopped talking, and I noticed. I guess I looked at him, and I must have still looked happy about what I was thinking. He was looking right at me. I think he thought I was proud of him or something. So he smiled at me and said, 'I wish you were my dad.' Then he cracked up, because that was kind of clever. He probably stole it from some movie. But I knew he meant it. And I thought, I suck. I really, really suck. Then I hit the phone pole."

"Sad story," Fred says.

"Yeah, and if by some miracle you remember that tomorrow, you'll have everything you need to get me off your back."

Fred shuts his eyes. He tightens them. "You said your kid was in the accident with you," he says.

"Remember that."

"Well, that's something," he says. He either looks at me or tries. "You know, if we were friends . . ." Then he raises his glass so I can see it's almost full. He smiles, toasts me, and drinks until the glass is just a tinkling bell. "Who the fuck am I kidding?"

"Seriously, what would you do?"

"I already did it," he says. "Bette said if I pulled out of the TV thing, she'd make sure you didn't take my yard, so I did. See, I'm a nice guy."

"Thanks."

"Yeah," he says. "You remember that. Because I won't."

* * *

Jim's game, v.4, 11:46: When the bear regained my consciousness, it was four A.M. my time. We were standing on the fringe of a garden, circular and akin to Versailles in its elegance, and isolated from the other levels by crumbling walls like a castle's backyard. Its fussy cobblestone paths were cartoon classical, but the flower beds were pure Rose Parade float, and the whole property was as shiny as a contact lens. The drafty sky was juggling some birds or loose kites and looked about a hue this side of storming. Whistling chimpanzees in baggy overalls were scattered through the foliage, raking and weeding. The maze of paths led and misled to a central oasis of sorts where we could barely see a kind of jungle gym of spurting turquoise water. I chose one path arbitrarily. White rabbits skittered by our feet and tried to trip the bear. I had him kick one of them to death out of vague curiosity, but its lifeless body forked over a fluttering rainbow trout, and we have a bunch of those. So I let the other rabbits live and watched our step. Things were cool until a groundskeeper noticed the bear and freaked out. He charged us, screeching and swinging the rake, but when the bear yelled we were God, he skidded to a halt and hid the weapon behind his back. Something I've noticed in our travels is that these multiples who guard most of the levels' ground floors are clones, and I don't mean just physically. They're knee-jerk psychopaths who quick-change into brusque, brown-nosing yes-men. They remind me of those slumming actor types who treat their day jobs like a David Mamet play. They schmooze God as if we were flashing an American Express Gold card, which I would find insulting if my bear aspect weren't so undiscerning. I keep reminding myself that I'm in costume, and if I want to make connections, I need to stay focused and defer to my appearance. Still, I can imagine how desperately those scientists searching the *Titanic* in their mini-submarines wished they were snorkeling. I let the bear have a pleasant conversation with his obsequious acquaintance until the fool thought he was God's new best friend. Then I threw a little wrath his way, and sure enough, he de-clenched into a lowlife snitch. He stammered out directions to the fountain and told us how to grab and turn some statues there until they faced north. This would drain the all-important fountain. We were to jump down some hole camouflaged into its pipes and mechanisms. He didn't know what awaited us below, but he was sure it would be evil and offer no competition for God. Maybe I'm losing it, but I swear I either saw or imagined a look of concern cross his otherwise hysterical face, which either touched me or caused me to pretend the bear was touched. All I know is, I felt an 'aw shucks' vibe pass through our character. After that, the walk to the fountain was nonsense. News of our deity status appeared to have spread throughout the kingdom by whatever telepathic means the game employs. By the time we reached that overly symmetrical fountain, the bear had accrued a little army of admiring rabbits, lozenge-like turtles, and multi-legged insect-sized thingies. They trailed behind us, spangling and whirring like paparazzi cameras that had fallen on the ground and grown legs. We stomped a few, hoping the rest of them would scatter, but nothing budged. These deaths also gave the bear some stocking stuffers we could have lived without. Up close, the fountain looked and sounded very fake, if that's not too great an oxymoron. The water was as clotted as a necklace, yet so acrobatic I'd swear its designer had never drunk a drop. The fountain's faux marble base was flanked by several statues of hypnotized-looking bears, all with perfect posture and recently brushed coats. They depicted us, no question about it. Still, unless they'd been carved after the God fad began, which seemed impossible, they made no sense at all. But again, I'm an absolute klutz with new technology—I can barely check my e-mail. Regardless, the bear hugged each statue and revolved it inch by inch until they faced this tidal wave of an untrimmed hedge, which we'd been guaranteed lay north. Suddenly, there was nothing in the fountain but dripping spouts, a few counterfeit coins, and a round drain, precisely carved out and black as a period. Before we jumped in, I did a zoom-scan number on the level. Apart from a rickety greenhouse with smudged or steamed-up windows that I later regretted not exploring, and those hick chimpanzees grinning and waving like midwesterners at a *Letterman* taping, the area seemed clear. So I walked the bear to the hole and off the edge. We crash-landed at the bottom of a brick well. There was a shallow pool of jellied so-called water at our feet, but otherwise it seemed a decent simulation of the kinds of wells I've seen dead kids get fished from on the news. But then bricks startled flying off the walls. They barely missed us and landed in a pile, then continued to collect until the pile was slightly taller than the bear. Two of the bricks paved themselves into rectangular eyeballs. A grumbling voice, presumably the pile's, announced that the bear had two minutes to replace every brick or else. That 'else' was left eerily vague, although it wasn't hard to guess there'd be a cave-in, since the well sounded awful, as if it were grinding its teeth. Then a digital clock face popped up in one corner of the screen and started devouring our time. I used a second to compose myself, then had the bear reveal that we were God as nonchalantly as he could. The pile didn't blink. The bear commanded the pile to re-place the bricks or else. The pile was deaf or un-moved. Even if God had been some latent day laborer, I had no clue which button made the bear fill blanks, nor did I recall or even really care which brick went where. I've never completed a jigsaw puzzle in my life. So we were forced into a macho standoff. The pile and bear just stood there, furry poker face to stony red facade, glancing up at the clock until our seconds were down to single digits. Then the pile cracked, or, to be more accurate, rap-idly disassembled brick by brick. They jetted every which way until the walls were relatively solid and claustrophobic again. Where the pile had stood, there was a Zippo lighter balanced on one corner and spinning like an Olympic athlete's ice skate. We walked toward it and, ding-a-ling, it reappeared

flaming in our paw. The well had never been real-
istically dark to begin with, nor was it that much
brighter now. There was nothing flammable in
view, and I was not about to turn us into protesting
monks. I guess we stood there dumbfounded for a
tiresome stretch of time because the well finally
grumbled something. We said, Excuse me? Bomb,
it said very wearily. Meaning what? we said. Well,
to make a long story short, we'd fucked up royally
by not checking out that greenhouse. Apparently,
it was not only quote-unquote a blast and far more
labyrinthine than it looked, but bombs grew there
in flourishes, and we could have plucked a few. Our
laziness triggered a jargon-filled lecture on game
strategy that concluded with the news that unless we
quit the game and started over, we'd be standing there
so long we'd make King Tut seem like Evel Knievel.
I knew in my soul that the God jig was up. So I lev-
eled with the well. That's to say, I had the bear rattle
off my whole sob story, from the car crash to the
terrible injustice of our current imprisonment. In

retrospect, its Mr. Spock–like logic shouldn't have surprised me. It was just a fake hole in fake ground, for heaven's sake, and our helpful plant friend had warned us not to ask for much from the 'movement-impaired,' as it described them, who formed the blue-collar workers of the game. Still, at the time, I hoped its walls might spring a leak or two in some surreal takeoff on sympathy. Instead, it rather bluntly explained that it had no idea what I was whining about. It said, 'Think about it this way. If I were a nail, and the bear were a hammer, then why the hell would I care about the carpenter?' Still, the well said it would allow our passage onward because that option was less irksome than playing upset stomach for the rest of its existence. The bear felt incredibly relieved, and even did one of his patented two-steps, but I knew better. Even then I could hear the rising falsetto din of infuriated creatures spreading word of our betrayal in the garden above. Luckily, just as the rakes and insects started raining on our head, a loosely-door-shaped section of the well collapsed. We ambled through a rosy cloud of demolished brick debris, then used the Zippo to negotiate our way toward a craggy bit of natural-looking light until we emerged in level six. By then it was almost noon my time. I could hear Bette's psychic prattling in the kitchen and knew he was about to swipe my bedroom. I felt tired and ill equipped to face whatever trauma my demystified bear had coming. At least we put a lot of tiny miles behind us, and I'm burnt beyond belief.

* * *

The psychic has petted Tommy's snow globes as if they were cats. He has leafed through every issue of *Thrasher* as if it were a fragile first edition. Now he's checking Tommy's rock collectibles. He takes each action figure from the shelf and clutches it like his Academy Award. Some, say Ozzy Osbourne, get lengthy Best Actor squeezes. Others, say what's-his-name from Green Day, get little more than a handshake. I'm watching from the unmade bed, still barely shy of human form. That's to say, I feel more hopeful than he warrants; I might have played the game so long my mind picked up a bug. Bette cleared out to give the guy his space, but some part of me would like his trinket if he has one.

*   *   *

"Ouch, that hurt," says the psychic. He jams Metallica's drummer into its pint-sized drum set. "Tommy's here. He's embarrassed. No, he's laughing at that poster right there." The psychic grips his fancy tripod canes and slowly clomps toward the defaced, slightly grainy Tony Hawk. He plants one cane, finds his balance, and starts massaging the poster. "May I ask its significance?"

"You know full well that's almost him."

"There's a lot coming up around you," says the psychic. His eyes glaze, then scrub me or some haze in my vicinity. "Your son is quite the extrovert, isn't he?"

"He liked to make himself known, yeah. So what's he saying?"

"I don't hear words," says the psychic. "If you follow baseball, imagine Randy Johnson's pitching and I'm at home plate. Except he isn't throwing baseballs but little pieces of my past. Flowers I bought my wife, my favorite junk food, a TV commercial from my childhood. It's up to me to figure out which ones are strikes."

"So the typing thing's a scam?"

"I said I don't hear words," says the psychic. "Apparently, dead people can't enunciate. Why they can type, I don't know. Perhaps it's that they know how to operate our bodies. Perhaps some of our more inexplicable acts and illnesses and accidents are their doing. Perhaps when murderers insist they weren't themselves, they're telling the truth."

"So how come you know they're using you and other people don't?"

"There's no other explanation," says the psychic. "I'm quite a boring, mainstream person. I have a

Labrador retriever named Labby. Channeling the dead is just completely out of character. Now, you . . . you're far more creative than I am. Perhaps when Tommy operates you, you mistakenly credit yourself."

"I used to think building that monument next door was just me fabricating Tommy's wish."

"For example," says the psychic.

"Or he could have paralyzed me, which seems more likely."

"Or cured you," says the psychic.

"Paralyzing makes more sense. If he did cure me, it's probably because he got bored of mind-fucking a cripple."

"I don't believe the dead get bored," says the psychic. "I think they're very Zen about the whole thing."

"The whole thing being what, in your opinion?"

"Well, I can tell you what they've shown me when I've asked," says the psychic. "For instance, I'm a bit of a DVD nut. Spaghetti westerns, if you happen to have any lying around. Well, you know those little extras? Deleted scenes, making-of documentaries, and so on? I've been shown a lot of those. One thing they've never shown me is the sky. No religious paintings, no science fiction movies, no oceans of fire. So my guess is whatever death involves, it's no picnic."

"Have you ever asked Tommy?"

"You really haven't read his messages, have you?" says the psychic.

"Not so far."

"Well, I'd rather not paraphrase him," says the psychic. "But I do think you should read them. You're topic number one."

"Is he still throwing stuff at you?"

"Yes, he is," says the psychic. "In fact, he seems to be enjoying our talk. I've been getting pom-poms for about a minute now. You wouldn't know it, but I was a cheerleader in high school. So let's just say he's throwing nasty little strikes. Okay, he just threw my laptop. There it is again. I'd better get to work, if you don't mind. Something all dead people seem to have in common is no patience with me whatsoever."

*   *   *

I'm reading Tommy's controversial notes from the supposed beyond. Actually, I just hurled them half-way across the room. Bette is in the kitchen reading his latest and crying her eyes out. I'm just one raspy breath away from joining her, which I think would save our marriage, but it won't come out. I never cried when Tommy was alive, I don't believe. He didn't, either, to my knowledge. Not that I was with him every second. His eyes would moisten when he blew his tournaments or broke a bone. I knew he couldn't help it, so I never saw that pair of his eyes as especially mysterious. Mostly, he let his legs do his emoting and expected me to figure out what their clumsiness implied. Or else he didn't care. Or maybe he didn't feel much, unless you count horny. I never thought there was much of me in him. I guess since he died, there's been a ton of him in me. Or that's what the notes keep insisting. He's still with me. He's always here with me. Don't ever worry that he's not here. But apart from our names, a vaguely two-story house, and its address, "here" could be anywhere. There's no smidgen of the monument. There are hundreds of typos but no car crash. Are dead kids so inhuman they would spam a fucked-up, lonely father? Is Bette so sentimental that form letters signed "Love, Tommy" make her cry? Are we really that dim?

* * *

I'm crouching in the monument. To unlock my version, you just grab the doorknob and pull. The workers dump their crap in here so it's full of soggy *Playboy*s and beer cans. The walls are wooden scaffolding that carve the insides into a splintery funnel. The floor's a stew of piss and footprints. There's no electricity or outlets, and I need my Zippo just to see around me. It's too cramped to stand inside, much less live in, much less fool some dead skater as a magical ramp. It wasn't meant to hide anything invaluable, or function at all, or even really be viewed. If Tommy is dictating creepy letters, or steering me where he wants . . . if Tommy cared about that building in the first place, and knows it was a waste of time to sneak his mind inside it . . . if all that's true, and only if, and that's such a massive if . . . I think I knew him superficially enough to understand what I would have to do to make this eyesore, quote, fucking awesome, end quote.

* * *

"Jim," Bette says. She's in the room with me. The game just loaded, but the bear's eyes are still polishing mine into spotlights. Her voice grates on him, and our name sounds so angry he tries to signal me to fight.

"What."

"The monument's on fire," she says. "Didn't you hear all the sirens?"

I look at her, and the bear peeks though my game face like a trick-or-treating kid. To him, she's long since solved and trinketless and just kind of plunked down on the carpet. "I'm sorry, what did you say?"

"Jim, listen," Bette says. "I said someone torched the monument." She plants herself between my fingers and their kingdom, which drains the goodness out of me.

"You're in my way."

"Have you completely lost it?" she says. Her eyes block mine and start to burrow. They're still a pretty blue, but such bullies, and I've seen prettier things. When Tommy died, she used to bully his grave. But it just lay there. She bullied my legs. She really missed our sex life, and they seemed stubborn at the time, but they were graves, too.

"It was probably Frank. Or some neighborhood kids."

"I imagine," Bette says. Then I guess she's dug around enough to see I'm rotten, because her eyes quit prying where they shouldn't. "If you can hear me, I want you out of here tomorrow."

*   *   *

The bear is walking in a sugarcoated, wizened-looking Alps. It's cozier than the real thing and even more slippery, like a clean toilet bowl. The mountainsides are flocked like Christmas trees, and strung with glinting, creaking chairlifts. The ground is packed with snow that has no temperature to speak of and sticks to our furry feet like sand. Each footstep cues a poorly synced crunch that the bear is mistaking for an echo. He feels at home, but I think he's more citified than he can realize. We just saw a polar bear not far ahead. It's only a cub wearing droopy hip-hop shorts, but I think I know a redneck when I see one. The bear wants to hightail it over, but I'm tugging on his leash to remind him I've lied and cheated.

* * *

'Tell the bear you're not going to kill us. I mean assuming you can't or won't. Because he thinks you're a friend.'

*   *   *

The little bear scrambles back a few steps. 'What are you?' he says. 'I have my opinion. I've heard the rumors. But I'd like to know the facts. Oh, you should know I'm an atheist. I'm not like the other idiotic cowards around here. I didn't believe in you before, and I really don't believe in you now.'

*   *   *

'Yeah, where is everybody? I expected ambush after ambush.'

*   *   *

'Hiding,' says the cub. 'They were fully into you until that bullshit yesterday. Not a big surprise, since there's nothing to do here. Just look around. God had their minds to yourself. They're not bad creatures, really.

They used to be, but it's been so long since there was anything to kill, they lost the taste. They're too nice, if anything. When they heard about God, they turned into these lazy-assed, do-nothing, navel-gazing pacifists. They thought imitating you would make them happy. The sad thing is, I guess it did. And the really sad thing is, now they think you're a deceitful, untrustworthy, selfish, weird God who's planning to trick them. So the good news for you is, I'm sure the evil snowman will pay you handsomely to take the mega-jump and leave this level undamaged. I hope you're happy. Me, I have to live with these messed-up freaks. Anyway, I repeat: What are you?'

* * *

'I'm a guy in a bear costume who's on a mission for my dead son. It's complicated. Anyway, I think you might have met him once. Tommy. This was originally his game. It's a long story, but he died, and I'm playing for him now.'

*   *   *

'Blah blah blah,' says the cub.

*   *   *

'I know dying's no big deal. I realize it's tantamount to a nap. But where I live, death's the end. It's erasure. It's so heavy we decide the dead are just invisible and mute. Death's so bad we'd rather go insane than know that one of us is nonexistent. That's me. The world I come from is huge and disorganized and no fun, and nothing there makes any of us happy. You'd melt like an ice cube. It's just constant pain and confusion like you couldn't imagine.'

*   *   *

'Blah blah blah,' says the cub. 'Look, when I hear stuff I don't understand, I blow it off. But I'm what they call young. I'm Mr. Undeveloped. The last time you came through here, I thought, Now, that bear's cool. You killed me. You killed everyone I know. You're my role model. When I heard you started hanging out a few levels over and wouldn't leave, I didn't think you were God. I thought you'd lost your edge. When I heard you were coming back, I thought you'd gotten cool again. When I heard about the whole 'dead, replaced, whatever' thing, I thought you were playing a prank. I was really looking forward to seeing you again. But you're not you, are you?'

*   *   *

'What would be so different if I were?'

*   *   *

'You'd kill me, duh,' says the cub. 'I'd be long gone. I'd be way past gore and revamping by now. You would have said, Fuck off, asshole. You would have said, You suck ass, you useless piece of shit. Those are exact quotes.'

* * *

'I really don't want to kill you, but I will, on one condition.'

* * *

'Seriously?' says the cub. 'I'll be triggered to attack, and that might bruise you, but I won't mean it. And when I die, you'll get an icicle. It'll return what I took.'

* * *

'Agreed, but first, where's that snowman you mentioned?'

* * *

'Just keep going straight,' says the cub. 'You can't miss the guy. He's mega. Okay, give me one second.' Then he steels his eyes until we see a tiny spark of hope. But his body senses prey and quickly covers his eyes with his claws. That makes me furious, I don't know why, like the time I told Bette I still loved her and she tossed her wedding ring into the garbage disposal. 'Now hit me with everything you've got. You can do it, loser. Just pretend I'm your son.'

*　　*　　*

Using the joystick as my bullwhip, I flog my bear. He resists and stands his ground until he knows my mind outweighs him. I think he'd rather whirl around and gut me, but his body's my knife. By then the cub has scraped us nearly bald and hit pay dirt. Pain turns the bear into a pragmatist. He averts his eyes and throws a single punch. It turns the cub into an illustrated dent. His fur coat crumples on the ground. It expends a crazy fractal that evaporates to mist. The mist hides his corpse and freezes stiff. A polar wind sculpts the block of ice into a pointy souvenir. The bear wishes he could keep it safe in a refrigerated pocket, or I do. But it dissolves through our footpads and gets quickly recycled into another nameless, mood-enhancing shard. If we could treasure it, I would.

When the snow looks like a sweater, and the crime scene's just a pinch, we journey onward. Apart from an intermittent headwind that redesigns us like an alphabet, and a very close call with some broken, flying tree limbs, it's a meditative, solitary nature hike of sorts. The bear deletes my outburst, or I absolve him, and soon enough the joystick's just his tilting spine again. With every foe well hidden under rocks, the bear and I are left to our devices. He concentrates on dodging icy streaks and starts to lose the bigger picture. I shut my eyes and disinfect him of my short, ungodlike temper. By the time I reopen them, we're both hopelessly lost.

*   *   *

Whenever I'm confused, the bear starts dawdling. He doesn't mind at first, but I'm a space case, and his patience does wear thin. He yawns, looks to his left then right, and gives his baggy ass a scratch. When he yawns, it's a contagion. Soon everything in sight has gotten bored of me, too. The wind machines grow unimaginative and tap out lazy breezes. The Old Faithful snowdrifts feel the rhythm and time-release their star-shaped props. The bear yawns and gives his ass another scrunch. Roughly eight seconds later, the bear, snow, and wind perform their simple tricks again. Together, they turn the game into a kind of outdoor concert. It's no Woodstock, but it's welcome, like when rock bands in their twilight used to entertain the troops, or like that screeching string quartet that made the sinking *Titanic* feel less obnoxious.

When I was young, I used to fantasize a lot. Like father like son, I suppose. But there were no X Games then, and I'd have married any actress I fucked. But I also thought the world was kind of tedious. Like every kid, I drew a lot of pictures, then beamed myself into them like the characters on *Star Trek*. Like every kid, I thought the world needed a face-lift, except the parts where Disney got there first. Tommy only liked Space Mountain, no surprise. But as a wuss, I needed more. For instance, no one could keep me off the Pirates of the Caribbean. I loved its merrymaking, unrelenting murders. I loved how every drunken, pistol-firing pirate was like a cuckoo clock with nonstop cuckoos. Then one time my boat got stuck inside the ride for hours. Afterward, that looping, scratched recording of a place became my hell. But I never blamed the pirates. And I never quite forgot how being shit-faced made them happy no matter whom their bullets hit. Maybe that's the reason I'm a pothead, or maybe not. All I'm thinking is this looping, violent game seems like a hell I would have loved.

DENNIS COOPER

* * *

'So you're God,' says a voice. It's omniscient or being broadcast in surround sound. It's loud, intensely so, but ingratiating, too, as if an earthquake were announcing a game show. The bear puts up his dukes, but I'm his designated driver. I crane his neck way back, and sure enough, one of the mountains is a fraud. It's a colossal stack of snowballs with huge bits of vegetation wedged into the highest, smallest ball to make a face.

* * *

'God's so minuscule,' says the snowman. 'But isn't everything—good, evil, and otherwise?'

* * *

'You must have quite the view. And if it's no trouble, could you try to keep it down?'

148

*   *   *

'Touché,' says the snowman. 'I'm supposed to make your ears ring. I can't do much about it. My voice is older than civilization. My whisper's worse. It would flip you like a quarter. But here's a thought. Try doing one of those amusing little dribbles. Right there where you're standing will work fine.'

*   *   *

I poke around until I find the combination. The bear goes airborne, does a Benihana, and cannonballs the snow into a foamy, sloshing tide pool. We sink up to our knees. Then the image crests and freezes, and the ground becomes our socks.

*   *   *

'Better, right?' says the snowman. I guess he's whispering. The volume's at a noisy-neighbor level, but every time he breathes, it slaps our face and twirls the bear's clumpy chest fur like propellers.

* * *

'Not bad.'

* * *

'Now, to answer your question,' says the snowman. 'I can see all the way to level one. I've seen just about everything that's ever happened. That's why I'm wiser than I look.'

* * *

'Then maybe you knew Tommy.'

* * *

'I've known all of you,' says the snowman. 'Some quite well, some by inference, and some like weathermen know forecasts. But you mean Tommy specifically? I killed that you twenty-seven times. You wanted the mega-jump, but you didn't earn it. You want to know how I kill? A picture's worth a thousand words, but nonetheless, I jump about yay high then squash you. It levels everything. You ought to see the crater. You ought to see your goo. Nasty doings. So, after twenty-seven wipeouts, you gave up and wandered back to level three. So began our little age of enlightenment. But I take no credit.'

* * *

'So Tommy was just a loser bear to you?'

* * *

'At the time, sure,' says the snowman. 'But remember, I was just a lion's share of pixels with a parrot's squawk back then. Compared to primordial me, your dinosaurs were a think tank. Anyway, now you're back, and I'm all grown up and ready to make amends. You name it. If I've got it, it's yours.'

* * *

'Well, what have you got?'

* * *

'Besides the mega-jump, I've got three nice cheats,' says the snowman. 'First, if you push the joystick forward and hold down R and L, you get to be invisible, but only in this level. That one's fun for sneak attacks, but considering the state of things, I wouldn't recommend it. Second, if you pull the joystick back and do a zoom on my face, then push B, I melt. But I regrow, so don't get greedy. That cheat's just silly. But if you hold down every button at the same time, you'll see a ladder on my back. It's there right now, but it's intangible. You'll have three minutes to make it to my head.

You probably can't see it, but I'm wearing a funny old top hat. It's just a crushed tin can to you. There's a coiled spring inside it, don't ask me how. If you reach the brim in time, the spring will send you flying. You can land almost anywhere you want, if you're not too picky. Just aim with the joystick as usual. Now, from what I can see going on in levels four and five, I recommend you use this third cheat and aim for level three, because paganism is running rampant, and you're a marked bear. But level three looks pretty mellow.'

* * *

'That sounds good. Speaking of level three, can you see a building there? It's—'

* * *

'Of course,' says the snowman. 'It's famously and inexplicably your favorite.'

*   *   *

'Since you're so wise, can you tell me what's inside it, or make an educated guess?'

*   *   *

'Okay, why are you doing this?' says the snowman. His big head starts to rotate very noisily. When the grinding stops, it's dangerously balanced on his second-smallest ball. Then he smiles at us a little too enthusiastically, like a preschooler's mural of the moon. "You're God. It's your call. The game's your fixer-upper. But it just seems kind of hostile.'

*   *   *

'You're changing the subject.'

*   *   *

'It's a puzzle,' says the snowman. 'I mean, what isn't? I mean, nickname it what you want. I'm not trying to be rude. It's just that when you see everything, you realize that nothing means anything.'

* * *

'You mean it's not a glitch?'

* * *

'You're the glitch,' says the snowman. 'I'm not referring to the bear. He fits in. He likes solving puzzles. He likes winning fights and getting gifts. We like being solved and getting killed and giving bears our gifts. I'm talking about you inside there. You and Tommy in particular. How long have you been working on that puzzle? For us, it's been centuries. This isn't the Giza Plateau, sir. Or should I say, I guess it is now, thanks to you. So you tell me. What does God think he's going to find in there, assuming you could solve it? And before you get your hopes up, the mega-jump won't help. Good try, though. You'll smash the bear to smithereens. You'll drizzle down that puzzle. No, it takes something else. You're not even warm.'

* * *

'Look, you guys are great. You give gifts the way clouds give raindrops. You're generosity incarnate. Still, your gifts are kind of shitty, to be honest. But imagine some serious, unbelievable gift. Imagine if, say, you could move, walk, drag yourself around the game, or whatever mobility means here. I'm talking go anywhere at any time.'

* * *

'Wow,' says the snowman. 'That's such a great gift, I'll feel depressed for the rest of my eternal winter knowing I can't get it.'

*   *   *

'I just know whatever's in there, it's important. Maybe something so great my son will ollie in his grave. Or maybe just some charming, empty house where I could live. This'll sound pathetic, but I kind of don't have anywhere to go. And before you remind me bears sleep in the woods or bring up drugs, I'm well aware I'm out of it. I know that wouldn't work. I'm too big and corporeal, et cetera. Just call it a weird combination of desperation and faith.'

*   *   *

'It's a honeycomb,' says the snowman. 'It's an extra-special, super-duper honeycomb, if that makes you feel better. It gives the bear infinite life. Kind of ironic, isn't it?'

*   *   *

'You're just saying that so I'll erase you. I know that's all you creatures want.'

* * *

'If only wisdom were that messy,' says the snowman. 'I miss my devious past. No, I tell the ugly truth. But if I might interject a little sanity, please do. And if I might be so bold, you did promise you would, if you remember. And if I might lift a page from your book, if you don't, I'm going to jump yay high and do the job myself. That's not devious, that's just called doing my thing. So take a minute. Consider that my prayer.'

* * *

We've won our standoffs in the past. Or enough of them to know our biggest draw is doing nothing. So I ignore the bear until he's just an itchy, yawning bore. But when the snowman's base starts smoking like a pad at Cape Canaveral, I panic. I wring and yank on the controller, but I might as well be a guy with a fishing pole trying to haul in Atlantis.

* * *

'Look, here's the deal. Tommy was my son. He liked that puzzle. I don't know why. He did a lot of drugs. So do I. Maybe that's the only reason. Now Tommy's dead. I loved Tommy. I think that's safe to assume. But he's gone, and that puzzle's still there. Whatever's in it meant a lot to him. Or it didn't. Probably it didn't. He was probably just stoned and bored and had nothing else to do. I'm probably just stoned and hiding out here in your game because my life is even more unsolvable than you. Imagine if every puzzle here, including you, was too difficult. Then imagine the miserable, boring bear you'd have to live with. That's what my life is like. My wife, my job, my friends, my house . . . you name it. Everything and everyone I know is either broken or locked so tight I can't break in. It's my fault. I accidentally killed my son, and I'm too scared or egotistical to face it. But you want to talk about a puzzle? Try making up a world where having killed someone you love isn't important.'

* * *

'Love sounds familiar,' says the snowman.

* * *

'Love's this thing you'd call the biggest prize in life. It's like that building or you, not to make your big head even bigger. You want to be inside that love, even if it's empty, and even if the ones who hide it are divorcing you or dead.'

* * *

'I was being sarcastic,' says the snowman. 'Don't worry. I get that all the time. It's my face. I've outgrown it.

Point is, I know love, or let's say I've read your mind.
We all have, ad infinitum. How do you suppose we
got our values? But we're a game, and you're the bear.
Big difference. We think, Enough already. You think,
I'll win. It happens all the time. The last time we met,
I let you walk. I let you turn a puzzle any child could
solve into the Sphinx. I let you turn my majestic view
into your blighted neighborhood. You want to know
about guilt? Still, the one good thing about us ivory
towers is we're smart enough to learn from your mis-
takes. How can I phrase this so you'll understand? Oh,
I know. Your son's dead.'

* * *

'Yeah, I know that.'

* * *

'Death doesn't hurt,' says the snowman. 'You just stop
moving. We'll just forget you. It'll be like you and

Tommy and the other bears were never even here. We'll all come back as fresh as babies. We'll love to see you. We'll let you kill us. We'll kill you. We won't know any better. Now, honestly, doesn't that sound nice?'

* * *

'Yeah, it does. Okay, quick, remind me how to do this.'

* * *

Let's say I've just erased the world and not destroyed mine. Let's say Marianne was right, and death's a fairy tale or game, and I've just buried my body near my son's. Let's say those little lamps and mats and scrims were trees and grass and mountains, and my real life was a game I didn't win. Let's say everything that didn't shine like glass was fake, and nothing made of glass had ever shattered, including my windshield. Let's say when Tommy died that night, he left a gift, however small. Let's say he gave me the power to erase the night I killed him and lost the game by accident. Let's say the extremely smooth grass in cemeteries is fake grass, and there is no one and nothing underneath it.